PUFFIN BOOKS

NOTHING TO BE AFRAID OF

Jan Mark grew up in Kent and attended the Canterbury College of Art, going on to teach art at Gravesend. She started her writing career in 1974, and has since written a large number of highly successful books, for which she has been awarded the Carnegie Medal and other prestigious prizes. Everything she does now is connected with books and writing, and she has spent two years as writer-in-residence at Oxford Polytechnic. She lives in Oxford.

NOTHING
TO BE AFRAID OF

by Jan Mark

Illustrated by David Parkins

PUFFIN BOOKS

PUFFIN BOOKS

Published by the Penguin Group
Penguin Books Ltd, 27 Wrights Lane, London W8 5TZ, England
Penguin Books USA Inc., 375 Hudson Street, New York, New York 10014, USA
Penguin Books Australia Ltd, Ringwood, Victoria, Australia
Penguin Books Canada Ltd, 10 Alcorn Avenue, Toronto, Ontario, Canada M4V 3B2
Penguin Books (NZ) Ltd, 182–190 Wairau Road, Auckland 10, New Zealand

Penguin Books Ltd, Registered Offices: Harmondsworth, Middlesex, England

First published by Kestrel Books 1980
Published in Puffin Books 1982
20 19 18 17 16 15 14 13 12

Copyright © Jan Mark, 1977, 1980
Illustrations copyright © David Parkins, 1980
All rights reserved

'The Coronation Mob' was originally commissioned
by the BBC in 1977, for the television series 'Jubilee
Jackanory', and was published the same year in a book
of that title

Printed in England by Clays Ltd, St Ives plc

For Isobel

WEST GRID STAMP					
NN		RR		WW	
NT		RT		WO	
NC		RC		WL	
NH		RB		WM	
NL		RP		WT	
NV		RS		WA	
NM		RW	1096	WR	
NB		RV		WS	
NE					
NP					

Contents

1 Nothing to be Afraid Of

'Robin won't give you any trouble,' said Auntie Lynn. 'He's very quiet.'

Anthea knew how quiet Robin was. At present he was sitting under the table and, until Auntie Lynn mentioned his name, she had forgotten that he was there.

Auntie Lynn put a carrier bag on the armchair.

'There's plenty of clothes, so you won't need to do any washing, and there's a spare pair of pyjamas in case – well, you know. In case . . .'

'Yes,' said Mum, firmly. 'He'll be all right. I'll ring you tonight and let you know how he's getting along.' She looked at the clock. 'Now, hadn't *you* better be getting along?'

She saw Auntie Lynn to the front door and Anthea heard them saying good-bye to each other. Mum almost told Auntie Lynn to stop worrying and have a good time, which would have been a mistake because Auntie Lynn was going up North to a funeral.

Auntie Lynn was not really an Aunt, but she had once been at school with Anthea's mum, and she was the kind of person who couldn't manage without a handle to her name; so Robin was not Anthea's cousin. Robin was not anything much, except four years old, and he looked a lot younger; probably because nothing ever happened to him. Auntie Lynn kept no pets that might give Robin germs, and never bought him toys that had sharp corners to dent him or wheels that could be swallowed. He wore balaclava helmets and bobble hats in winter to

9

protect his tender ears, and a knitted vest under his shirt in summer in case he overheated himself and caught a chill from his own sweat.

'Perspiration,' said Auntie Lynn.

His face was as pale and flat as a saucer of milk, and his eyes floated in it like drops of cod-liver oil. This was not so surprising as he was full to the back teeth with cod-liver oil; also with extract of malt, concentrated orange juice and calves-foot jelly. When you picked him up you expected him to squelch, like a hot-water bottle full of half-set custard.

Anthea lifted the tablecloth and looked at him.

'Hello, Robin.'

Robin stared at her with his flat eyes and went back to sucking his woolly doggy that had flat eyes also, of sewn-on felt, because glass ones might find their way into Robin's appendix and cause damage. Anthea wondered how long it would be before he noticed that his mother had gone. Probably he wouldn't, any more than he would notice when she came back.

Mum closed the front door and joined Anthea in looking under the table at Robin. Robin's mouth turned down at the corners, and Anthea hoped he would cry so that they could cuddle him. It seemed impolite to cuddle him before he needed it. Anthea was afraid to go any closer.

'What a little troll,' said Mum, sadly, lowering the tablecloth. 'I suppose he'll come out when he's hungry.'

Anthea doubted it.

Robin didn't want any lunch or any tea.

'Do you think he's pining?' said Mum. Anthea did not. Anthea had a nasty suspicion that he was like this all the time. He went to bed without making a fuss and fell asleep before the light was out, as if he were too bored to stay awake. Anthea left her bedroom door open, hoping that he would have a nightmare so that she could go in and comfort him, but Robin slept all night without a squeak, and woke in the morning as flat-faced as before. Wall-eyed Doggy looked more excitable than Robin did.

'If only we had a proper garden,' said Mum, as Robin went under the table again, leaving his breakfast eggs scattered round the plate. 'He might run about.'

Anthea thought that this was unlikely, and in any case they didn't have a proper garden, only a yard at the back and a stony strip in front, without a fence.

'Can I take him to the park?' said Anthea.

Mum looked doubtful. 'Do you think he wants to go?'

'No,' said Anthea, peering under the tablecloth. 'I don't think he wants to do anything, but he can't sit there all day.'

'I bet he can,' said Mum. 'Still, I don't think he should. All right, take him to the park, but keep quiet about it. I don't suppose Lynn thinks you're safe in traffic.'

'He might tell her.'

'Can he talk?'

Robin, still clutching wall-eyed Doggy, plodded beside her all the way to the park, without once trying to jam his head between the library railings or get run over by a bus.

'Hold my hand, Robin,' Anthea said as they left the house, and he clung to her like a lamprey.

The park was not really a park at all; it was a garden. It did not even pretend to be a park and the notice by the gate said KING STREET GARDENS, in case anyone tried to use it as a park. The grass was as green and as flat as the front-room carpet, but the front-room carpet had a path worn across it from the door to the fireplace, and here there were more notices that said KEEP OFF THE GRASS, so that the gritty white paths went obediently round the edge, under the orderly trees that stood in a row like the queue outside a fish shop. There were bushes in each corner and one shelter with a bench in it. Here and there brown holes in the grass, full of raked earth, waited for next year's flowers, but there were no flowers now, and the bench had been taken out of the shelter because the shelter was supposed to be a summer-house, and you couldn't have people using a summer-house in winter.

Robin stood by the gates and gaped, with Doggy depending limply from his mouth where he held it by one ear, between his teeth. Anthea decided that if they

12

met anyone she knew, she would explain that Robin was only two, but very big for his age.

'Do you want to run, Robin?'

Robin shook his head.

'There's nothing to be afraid of. You can go all the way round, if you like, but you mustn't walk on the grass or pick things.'

Robin nodded. It was the kind of place that he understood.

Anthea sighed. 'Well, let's walk round, then.'

They set off. At each corner, where the bushes were, the path diverged. One part went in front of the bushes, one part round the back of them. On the first circuit Robin stumped glumly beside Anthea in front of the bushes. The second time round she felt a very faint tug at her hand. Robin wanted to go his own way.

This called for a celebration. Robin could think. Anthea crouched down on the path until they were at the same level.

'You want to walk round the back of the bushes, Robin?'

'Yiss,' said Robin.

Robin could *talk*.

'All right, but listen.' She lowered her voice to a whisper. 'You must be very careful. That path is called Leopard Walk. Do you know what a leopard is?'

'Yiss.'

'There are two leopards down there. They live in the bushes. One is a good leopard and the other's a bad leopard. The good leopard has black spots. The bad leopard has red spots. If you see the bad leopard you must say, "Die leopard die or I'll kick you in the eye," and run like anything. Do you understand?'

Robin tugged again.

'Oh no,' said Anthea. 'I'm going *this* way. If you want

13

to go down Leopard Walk, you'll have to go on your own. I'll meet you at the other end. Remember, if it's got red spots, run like mad.'

Robin trotted away. The bushes were just high enough to hide him, but Anthea could see the bobble on his hat doddering along. Suddenly the bobble gathered speed and Anthea had to run to reach the end of the bushes first.

'Did you see the bad leopard?'

'No,' said Robin, but he didn't look too sure.

'Why were you running, then?'

'I just wanted to.'

'You've dropped Doggy,' said Anthea. Doggy lay on the path with his legs in the air, halfway down Leopard Walk.

'You get him,' said Robin.

'No, *you* get him,' said Anthea. 'I'll wait here.' Robin moved off, reluctantly. She waited until he had recovered Doggy and then shouted, 'I can see the bad leopard in the bushes!' Robin raced back to safety. 'Did you say, "Die leopard die or I'll kick you in the eye"?' Anthea demanded.

'No,' Robin said, guiltily.

'Then he'll *kill* us,' said Anthea. 'Come on, run. We've got to get to that tree. He can't hurt us once we're under that tree.'

They stopped running under the twisted boughs of a weeping ash. 'This is a python tree,' said Anthea. 'Look, you can see the python wound round the trunk.'

'What's a python?' said Robin, backing off.

'Oh, it's just a great big snake that squeezes people to death,' said Anthea. 'A python could easily eat a leopard. That's why leopards won't walk under this tree, you see, Robin.'

Robin looked up. 'Could it eat us?'

'Yes, but it won't if we walk on our heels.' They walked on their heels to the next corner.

'Are there leopards down there?'

'No, but we must never go down there anyway. That's Poison Alley. All the trees are poisonous. They drip poison. If one bit of poison fell on your head, you'd die.'

'I've got my hat on,' said Robin, touching the bobble to make sure.

'It would burn right through your hat,' Anthea assured him. 'Right into your brains. *Fzzzzzzz.*'

They by-passed Poison Alley and walked on over the manhole cover that clanked.

'What's that?'

'That's the Fever Pit. If anyone lifts that manhole cover, they get a terrible disease. There's this terrible disease down there, Robin, and if the lid comes off, the disease will get out and people will die. I should think there's enough disease down there to kill everybody in this town. It's ever so loose, look.'

'Don't lift it! Don't lift it!' Robin screamed, and ran to the shelter for safety.

'Don't go in there,' yelled Anthea. 'That's where the Greasy Witch lives.' Robin bounced out of the shelter as though he were on elastic.

'Where's the Greasy Witch?'

'Oh, you can't see her,' said Anthea, 'but you can tell where she is because she smells so horrible. I think she must be somewhere about. Can't you smell her now?'

Robin sniffed the air and clasped Doggy more tightly.

'And she leaves oily marks wherever she goes. Look, you can see them on the wall.'

Robin looked at the wall. Someone had been very busy, if not the Greasy Witch. Anthea was glad on the whole that Robin could not read.

'The smell's getting worse, isn't it, Robin? I think we'd better go down here and then she won't find us.'

'She'll see us.'

'No, she won't. She can't see with her eyes because they're full of grease. She sees with her ears, but I expect they're all waxy. She's a filthy old witch, really.'

They slipped down a secret-looking path that went round the back of the shelter.

'Is the Greasy Witch down here?' said Robin, fearfully.

'I don't know,' said Anthea. 'Let's investigate.' They tiptoed round the side of the shelter. The path was damp and slippery. 'Filthy old witch. She's certainly *been* here,' said Anthea. 'I think she's gone now. I'll just have a look.'

She craned her neck round the corner of the shelter. There was a sort of glade in the bushes, and in the middle was a stand-pipe, with a tap on top. The pipe was lagged with canvas, like a scaly skin.

'Frightful Corner,' said Anthea. Robin put his cautious head round the edge of the shelter.

'What's that?'

Anthea wondered if it could be a dragon, up on the tip of its tail and ready to strike, but on the other side of the bushes was the brick back wall of the King Street Public Conveniences, and at that moment she heard the unmistakable sound of a cistern flushing.

'It's a Lavatory Demon,' she said. 'Quick! We've got to get away before the water stops, or he'll have us.'

They ran all the way to the gates, where they could see the church clock, and it was almost time for lunch.

Auntie Lynn fetched Robin home next morning, and three days later she was back again, striding up the path like a warrior queen going into battle, with Robin dangling from her hand, and Doggy dangling from Robin's hand.

Mum took her into the front room, closing the door. Anthea sat on the stairs and listened. Auntie Lynn was in full throat and furious, so it was easy enough to hear what she had to say.

'I want a word with that young lady,' said Auntie Lynn. 'And I want to know what she's been telling him.' Her voice dropped, and Anthea could hear only certain fateful words: 'Leopards . . . poison trees . . . snakes . . . diseases!'

Mum said something very quietly that Anthea did not hear, and then Auntie Lynn turned up the volume once more.

'Won't go to bed unless I leave the door open . . . wants the light on . . . up and down to him all night . . . won't go to the bathroom on his own. He says the – the – ,' she hesitated, 'the *toilet* demons will get him. He nearly broke his neck running downstairs this morning.'

Mum spoke again, but Auntie Lynn cut in like a band-saw.

'Frightened out of his wits! He follows me everywhere.'

The door opened slightly, and Anthea got ready to bolt, but it was Robin who came out, with his thumb in his mouth and circles round his eyes. Under his arm was soggy Doggy, ears chewed to nervous rags.

Robin looked up at Anthea through the bannisters.

'Let's go to the park,' he said.

2 Charming!

Alice and Lydia Pitt were saving up for a padlock. In the meantime they had to rely on the power of fear to keep people out of the garden shed across the lane. Alice had pinned a notice on the door:

CAUTION
DEADLY SPIRITS

The Pitts lived in the garden flat, which was right at the bottom of the house, down the area steps, so the shed was officially theirs, but the lane that ran along the ends of the gardens was a right-of-way. Anybody could walk down it, and the sheds were on the other side. The rest of the sheds had bolts and chains and keys, but Mrs Pitt said there was nothing in the shed worth stealing, so why waste good money? Alice and Lydia kept quiet. There *had* been nothing in the shed worth stealing, but there was something now. They put threepenny bits in a jam jar – on the rare occasions that they came by a three-penny bit.

'Why don't you ask your daddy to buy you one?' said Maureen, who was poking about uninvited in Alice's bedside cupboard and had discovered the jam jar. Alice and Lydia kept quiet about that, too. If their father was buying anything, it wasn't for them. They could not quite remember when they had last seen him. Lydia thought it was on Bonfire Night, but Lydia was only six. Alice knew that it was not last Bonfire Night, or even the one before that.

Alice's bedside cupboard, and Lydia's, were made

out of orange-boxes, as were the bookcases in the front room and the shelves in the kitchen. Mrs Pitt, who could sew, had made covers and curtains to fit the orange-boxes. One, lying on its side under the window, had a padded top. Alice could sit there to read by the little light that came down the area steps, and Lydia kept her toys inside it.

Mrs Pitt sewed things for other people too, if they asked her, in between cleaning other people's houses and looking after other people's children. While she was out doing all this, Alice looked after Lydia.

Lydia thought that everyone lived this way and didn't mind, but Alice knew differently and often felt badly about it, especially when Maureen came round to play. Maureen liked going down the area steps and knocking at the green door underneath; she liked the darkness at noon down there, below the road; and she admired the dear little orange-box cupboards with frills on. All the same, she would not have liked to be Alice Pitt and live there all the time. Lydia had never lived anywhere else. She was pale and wide-eyed, like something raised under a stone, according to Gregory Beasley's mother. Lydia was thought to be a bit strange. She certainly looked it.

'Let's go and play in the garden,' said Maureen, one summer's day at half past two, when it became too dark in the front room to see even the darns on Alice's cardigan. They went outside and Maureen continued to poke about.

'What's all that green stuff all over the lawn?' she demanded. It was nice of her to call it a lawn. It grew in lumps.

'Spinach,' said Alice.

Maureen began to giggle.

'Why've you got spinach on the lawn?'

'Mum planted it in the flowerbeds last year,' said Alice, 'but we didn't cut all of it in time and it seeded. Now it's everywhere.'

'I'm fed up with spinach,' said Lydia, and daringly wasteful she grubbed up a handful and threw it over the fence.

'You don't eat it, do you?' said Maureen.

'Why not? We can't afford to leave it,' Alice said, sharply.

'But it's wild. Look, it's even growing on the path. It's growing on the rubbish heap. Ugh!'

'It's still spinach.'

Maureen leaned on the fence at the end of the short garden and looked across the muddy lane.

'"Caution deadly spirits." What have you got in that old shed, anyway?'

'It's my laboratory,' said Alice.

Maureen laughed, but not too loudly. Alice Pitt might not have tuppence to bless herself with, but she had plenty between the ears.

'And plenty behind them,' said Gregory Beasley's mother.

'Nonsense. Those two girls are kept spotless,' said Maureen's mother, who liked to be nice about Mrs Pitt.

Gregory Beasley shared his mother's opinion, but the one time Gregory had leaned over the area railings yelling, 'Stinky old Alice, hasn't got a palace. Cess Pitt. Cess Pitt!' Alice herself had come up the steps and given him such a kick that he never dared tell his mates what had lamed him.

'What do you do in a laboratory?' said Maureen.

'I invent things,' said Alice, who spent as much time as she could at the Public Library, educating herself, since she didn't trust her teacher to do it.

'I want everyone in the class to write an essay about

his or her favourite ambition,' said Miss Cornwell. Alice very truthfully wrote about saving up for a pad-lock. 'I meant your ambition when you leave school, dear,' said Miss Cornwell, and gave her two out of ten. 'Silly old moo-cow,' said Alice, under her breath.

'What do you invent?' said Maureen. 'Machines?'

'Potions,' said Alice. 'Herbal remedies.'

'What's a remedy?'

'Medicine and things to put on your skin.' There was a herbalist's shop near the cinema, and Alice enjoyed looking in the window at the jars and white paper packets and cakes of lavender soap, made from real lavender. When she had achieved the padlock, she intended to start saving for some basic ingredients.

'Medicine shouldn't be deadly,' Maureen said, reasonably.

'It isn't,' said Alice, 'but I had to think of something that would keep people out.'

'I should think it would make people want to look inside,' said Maureen.

'I know.' Alice sighed. She had seen Gregory Beasley lurking.

'Can *I* see inside?'

'All right. But you mustn't touch anything and you mustn't tell.'

'What'd you do if I did?' said Maureen. 'Put a spell on me?'

'I'd kick you,' said Alice. Alice's kicks were famous. 'And I won't get you any more library books.' Alice had access to the whole family's library tickets, including her father's, and Maureen was grateful for the loans. Maureen's mother would not let her go to the library in case she met nasty men on the way, in the Memorial Gardens where there were bushes.

'Alice never meets any nasty men,' said Maureen.

'Alice kicks,' said Maureen's mother.

Alice opened the door of the shed. Inside were shelves and cobwebs, grey and thick as floorcloths, and leaning towers of flowerpots. The little cracked window was so dirty that everything outside looked brown, like an old photograph. Half a bicycle hung from the rafters, beside a watering-can with a potmender in the bottom, and along one wall was a bench with the remains of a vice screwed to it. The bench had been thoroughly dusted and scrubbed, and ranged on it were jars, and bottles and little cold-cream pots.

'It stinks,' said Maureen. 'It's all filthy. Mummy would skin me if she knew I was here.'

'Don't tell her, then,' said Lydia. Maureen ignored her. She had no intention of telling her mother that she had been in Alice Pitt's back shed, but she thought it would do Alice no harm to know that she was breaking rules on Alice's behalf.

'It only smells of creosote,' said Alice. 'There's a can of it down there.'

Maureen looked under the bench.

'Where'd you get all this stuff?'

'It was here when we moved in,' said Alice. She closed the door and lit a candle. The shed was dusty-dark, and warm.

'A lot of those things are poisonous,' said Maureen, seeing weedkiller and paraffin and anonymous rusty cans with conical tops. 'They aren't your medicines, are they? You could kill people.'

'No I couldn't,' said Alice. 'My things are all up here.' She put down the candle on the bench and pointed to the row of jars. Maureen peered.

'What's all that in there? Rose petals?'

'Yes.'

'What are you going to do with them?'

'Make scent,' said Alice.

'Aren't they a pretty colour – hey! You pinched them off Dr Hardy's roses, didn't you?' Dr Hardy lived in the next road, and his long garden stretched halfway down it. Rose bushes hung over the fence.

'I didn't pinch them,' said Alice. 'But you know how they get when they open right up, all loose? Well, if you hold out your hands underneath and breathe hard, all the petals drop off and you can catch them. They'd just fall on the ground, otherwise, and people would squash them,' she added, rationally.

'I got little red ones,' said Lydia.

'She threw them all up in the air,' said Alice.

'It was like weddings,' said Lydia.

'It was a terrible waste,' said Alice. 'We put some out on a tray to dry for pot-pourri, but it got windy while we were out shopping, and they'd all blown away, time we got back. They were wasted, too.'

'Well, what are you going to do with those?' said Maureen, pointing to the petals in the jar. 'They don't smell like scent to me. They smell like – vinegar.'

'I did put some vinegar in. Vinegar preserves things. I had to see if it would work,' said Alice. 'But it didn't.'

'I like these.' Maureen fiddled about with the cold-cream jars. 'Where'd you get them from?'

'Rubbish heaps,' said Alice. 'You can nearly always find cold-cream jars on rubbish heaps. And whelk shells. I don't know why. I'm making face-cream.'

'What with? Not real cream?'

'No. Dripping and cucumber mostly, and bluebell seeds; and mignonette.'

'Bluebell seeds and *dripping*?'

'I got the recipe out of an old book. It's supposed to be lard, but we haven't got any. Dripping's near enough,' said Alice. 'I thought the bluebell seeds might make it smoother. They're all gluey when you pop them.'

'I never tried,' said Maureen.

'The mignonette's to make it smell nice. Cucumber's right, though,' said Alice. 'It did say cucumber.'

Maureen unscrewed the lid from one of the little pots and discovered a mouldy puddle inside, the colour of old kerbstones.

'I have to experiment,' said Alice, defensively. 'Inventions never come right the first time. It took years to discover penicillin. And it's so hard to get things to put in,' she added sadly. 'No one round here grows herbs.'

'It's not really herbs, is it?' said Maureen, hurriedly replacing the lid. 'I don't think mignonette's a herb. Cucumbers aren't herbs.'

'Mint's a herb. We've got mint all over – where it isn't spinach. I put some in a lotion – '

'Potion?'

'No, lotion. With dock leaves. I thought it might be good for nettle stings.'

Maureen did not bother to ask if the lotion had been a success.

'You can eat nettles,' said Lydia, suddenly.

'Like spinach,' Maureen jeered.

'Mrs Witkowski told me.'

'Mrs Witkowski's *foreign*.'

'I suppose,' Alice said, diffidently, 'I suppose your mum hasn't got any old jars?'

'Jam jars?'

'No, this sort. Little make-up jars. My mum doesn't wear make-up.'

'I'll ask her,' said Maureen. Alice's mum didn't even put her hair in curlers. Poor Alice.

*

'Jars for Alice?' said Maureen's mother. 'Is she going to sell them? I gave all ours to that Scout who came round collecting.'

'Not jam jars,' said Maureen. 'I meant those little glass white ones with face things in, or Daddy's Brylcreem jars. She plays with them.'

'I would have thought Alice was a bit old to be playing with jars,' said Maureen's mother. 'Don't you mean Lydia? She's too young to be playing with glass.'

'She doesn't play like *that*,' said Maureen. 'She invents things and puts them in jars, like make-up. It's only pretend.'

Maureen suspected that if Alice had been able to get hold of the things she needed, there would have been less experiment and no need for pretence. Her mother fetched out some jars and an old cut-glass scent bottle as a treat.

'It's slightly chipped on this side. Tell her to be careful.'

Maureen would have liked the little bottle for herself. With the stopper out it still smelled pretty, but she knew that one ought to be kind to Alice, and handed it over with the jars.

Alice was very pleased and gave Maureen some pink lip-salve made of squashed geranium petals.

'It's not poisonous, but you'll have to use it up quickly, or it goes a funny colour,' said Alice, pounding nasturtium leaves with the handle of a trowel.

'Lots of lipsticks do that,' said Maureen, generously. 'I saw it in *Woman's Own*.'

'Alice put her ocean on my nettle sting and it went away,' said Lydia.

'*Lotion*,' said Alice.

'Maureen could put your ocean on her wart.'

'I haven't got a wart,' said Maureen.

'Yes you have. I saw,' said Lydia.

'Let's have a look,' said Alice, wiping her hands on her apron, very professional.

'I haven't *got* a wart.'

'It's on her thumb.'

'Shut up, Lyddy. You go on with the nasturtiums,' said Alice, prising Maureen's clenched thumb away from her palm. 'It's a big one, isn't it?'

'I keep knocking it. Mummy put caustic on, but it won't go away. Gregory Beasley said you get warts off being dirty,' said Maureen, pink with shame.

'Gregory Beasley thinks everybody's dirty,' said Alice feelingly.

'Gregory Beasley does things behind the shed,' said Lydia, in a faraway voice. 'I saw.'

'Did your nettle lotion really work?' Maureen asked, hopefully. 'The caustic didn't.'

'It only works on nettles,' said Alice. 'I'll have to charm this.'

'Don't be daft.'

'It's not daft. It's not half as daft as some of this lot,' said Alice, shrugging at the laboratory. 'I had three on my finger, and my gran charmed them away. It really works.'

'I bet it doesn't.'

'Won't do any harm to try, will it?' said Alice. 'It won't cost you. That's better than spending good money on caustic pencils that don't work, isn't it?'

'Caustic doesn't cost much.'

'*We* couldn't afford it,' said Alice. 'Charming's got to be done free or you lose the power, but you'll have to steal something.'

'I'm not stealing anything,' said Maureen. 'Mummy wouldn't like it.'

'Mummy wouldn't like it,' chanted Lydia, in her little, little voice.

'What'd I have to steal?'

'A bit of meat.'

'You steal it.'

'We haven't got any meat,' said Alice. 'It's baked beans and bacon today. I don't think bacon would work.'

'Chops on Saturday,' said Lydia, happily.

'You can't take bits off chops,' said Alice. 'Anyway, Mum would notice. Anyway, it's your wart, Maureen, and you have meat every day.'

'There's some beef in the pantry.'

'That'll do. Rolled up?'

'No, all floppy. I could get a bit of that.'

'It needn't be a very big piece, not just for the one wart. Is your Mum home, Maureen?'

'Shopping.'

'Go on, then.'

'I think it's silly,' said Maureen, but she went home and returned to the shed ten minutes later, with a little bit of raw beef wrapped up in her handkerchief.

'Ugh. It's all bloody,' she said, unwrapping it. 'I'll have to tell my mother I had a nose bleed.'

'Of course it's all bloody. If it didn't have blood in it, it wouldn't be red, would it?' said Alice. 'Give it here.' She took the meat and rubbed it carefully all round and over the wart.

'Ugh,' said Maureen, again. 'It's still there. Now what are you going to do?'

'Bury it,' said Alice.

'The wart?'

'The meat.'

'Come on, then,' said Maureen. 'Where shall we put it?'

'You mustn't know that, or it won't work.'

'All right. I won't look.'

'Oh no,' said Alice. 'You must go home and don't come back till it's gone.'

'You're just trying to get rid of me,' said Maureen. 'It won't go.'

'Yes it will, but you mustn't come back until it does.'

'I don't believe that.'

'It doesn't matter, as long as I do,' said Alice. Maureen began to be frightened, there in the dark shed beside solemn, raggedy Alice and batty Lydia, mumbling and pumping up and down like a little engine, with her trowel handle.

*

Three days later, Maureen woke up in the morning and found that the wart had gone. She went over to the bedroom window where the sun shone, and examined her thumb, but there was no sign at all of any wart; not even a scar.

'What are you doing?' said her mother, coming in with clean clothes.

'My wart's gone,' said Maureen.

'So it has. Fancy, after all this time.'

'Alice Pitt charmed it.'

'Don't be silly,' said Maureen's mother. 'It must have been the caustic.'

'Yes,' said Maureen.

'Wart-charming is a silly superstition. I don't want to hear any more nonsense like that.'

'No.'

'It was the caustic.'

'Yes,' said Maureen, but she didn't believe it. Mint-flavoured nettle lotion and grey face-cream were one thing; this was real. It had worked.

When she went down the road later, she saw Alice in the gutter, turning a rope for Lydia to jump over. 'Salt – mustard – vinegar – pepper. Salt – mustard – vinegar – pepper.' The other end of the rope was tied to the area railings.

'It's gone then,' said Alice, as Maureen drew close.

'How'd you know, clever-pot?' said Maureen.

'You wouldn't have come back, otherwise,' said Alice, calmly. 'Let's see.'

'I *would* have.'

'No.' Alice stopped swinging the rope and stood in the gutter, very sure of herself. 'I knew you wouldn't come back till it went.'

'I'm never coming back again, neither,' Maureen

shouted. 'You're horrible. I hate you!' And she ran home, crying.

'Funny,' said Alice. 'She didn't mind the geraniums, and they don't work at all, hardly.'

'That's why,' said Lydia.

Alice gazed long and hard at her little sister, but Lydia only stood on one leg, and scratched, and sucked her thumb, like anyone's little sister.

'Well,' Alice said finally, 'we'd better not tell her what *you* can do. Come on, Lyddy. *Salt* – mustard – vinegar – pepper. *Salt* – mustard – vinegar – pepper. *Salt* – mustard – vinegar – pepper . . . '

3 The Choice is Yours

The Music Room was on one side of the quadrangle and the Changing Room faced it on the other. They were linked by a corridor that made up the third side, and the fourth was the view across the playing-fields. In the Music Room Miss Helen Francis sat at the piano, head bent over the keyboard as her fingers tittuped from note to note, and swaying back and forth like a snake charming itself. At the top of the Changing Room steps Miss Marion Taylor stood, sportively poised with one hand on the doorknob and a whistle dangling on a string from the other; quivering with eagerness to be out on the field and inhaling fresh air. They could see each other. Brenda, standing in the doorway of the Music Room, could see them both.

'Well, come in, child,' said Miss Francis. 'Don't *haver*. If you must haver, don't do it in the doorway. Other people are trying to come in.'

Brenda moved to one side to make way for the other people, members of the choir who would normally have shoved her out of the way and pushed past. Here they shed their school manners in the corridor and queued in attitudes of excruciated patience. Miss Helen Francis favoured the noiseless approach. Across the quadrangle the Under-Thirteen Hockey XI roistered, and Miss Marion Taylor failed to intervene. Miss Francis observed all this with misty disapproval and looked away again.

'Brenda dear, are you coming in, or going out, or putting down roots?'

The rest of the choir was by now seated; first sopranos on the right, second sopranos on the left, thirds across one end and Miss Humphry, who was billed as an alto but sang tenor, at the other. They all sat up straight, as trained by Miss Francis, and looked curiously at Brenda who should have been seated too, among the first sopranos. Her empty chair was in the front row, with the music stacked on it, all ready. Miss Francis cocked her head to one side like a budgerigar that sees a millet spray in the offing.

'Have you a message for us, dear? From above?' She meant the headmistress, but by her tone it could have been God and his angels.

'No, Miss Francis.'

'From *beyond*?'

'Miss Francis, can I ask – ?'

'You *may* ask, Brenda. Whether or not you *can* is beyond my powers of divination.'

Brenda saw that the time for havering was at an end.

'Please, Miss Francis, may I be excused from choir?'

The budgie instantly turned into a marabou stork.

'Excused, Brenda? Do you have a pain?'

'There's a hockey practice, Miss Francis.'

'I am aware of that.' Miss Francis cast a look, over her shoulder and across the quadrangle, that should have turned Miss Taylor to stone, and the Under-Thirteen XI with her. 'How does it concern you, Brenda? How does it concern me?'

'I'm in the team, Miss Francis, and there's a match on Saturday,' said Brenda.

'But, my dear,' Miss Francis smiled at her with surpassing sweetness. 'I think my mind must be going.' She lifted limp fingers from the keyboard and touched them to her forehead, as if to arrest the absconding mind. 'Hockey practices are on Tuesdays and Fridays. Choir practices are on Mondays and Thursdays. It was ever thus. Today is Thursday. Everyone else thinks it's Thursday, otherwise they wouldn't be here.' She swept out a spare arm that encompassed the waiting choir, and asked helplessly, 'It *is* Thursday, isn't it? You all think it's Thursday? It's not just me having a little brainstorm?'

The choir tittered, *sotto voce*, to assure Miss Francis that it was indeed Thursday, and to express its mass contempt for anyone who was fool enough to get caught in the cross-fire between Miss Francis and Miss Taylor.

'It's a match against the High School, Miss Francis. Miss Taylor called a special practice,' said Brenda, hoping that her mention of the High School might save her, for if Miss Francis loathed anyone more than she loathed Miss Taylor, it was the music mistress at the High School. If the match had been against the High School choir, it might have been a different matter, and Miss Francis might have been out on the side-lines chanting with the rest of them: 'Two – four – six – eight, who – do – we – hate?'

Miss Francis, however, was not to be deflected. 'You know that I do not allow any absence from choir without a very good reason. Now, will you sit down, please?' She turned gaily to face the room. 'I think we'll begin with the Schubert.'

'Please. May I go and tell Miss Taylor that I can't come?'

Miss Francis sighed a sigh that turned a page on the music stand.

'Two minutes, Brenda. We'll wait,' she said venomously, and set the metronome ticking on the piano so that they might all count the two minutes, second by second.

Miss Taylor still stood upon the steps of the Changing Room. While they were all counting, they could turn round and watch Brenda tell Miss Taylor that she was not allowed to attend hockey practice.

Tock.

Tock.

Tock.

Brenda closed the door on the ticking and began to run. She would have to run to be there and back in two minutes, and running in the corridors was forbidden.

Miss Taylor had legs like bath loofahs stuffed into long, hairy grey socks, that were held up by tourniquets of narrow elastic. When she put on her stockings after school and mounted her bicycle to pedal strenuously home up East Hill, you could still see the twin red marks, like the rubber seals on Kilner jars. The loofahs were the first things that Brenda saw as she mounted the steps, and the grey socks bristled with impatience.

'Practice begins at twelve fifty,' said Miss Taylor. 'I suppose you were thinking of joining us?'

Brenda began to cringe all over again.

'Please, Miss Taylor, Miss Francis says I can't come.'

'Does she? And what's it got to do with Miss Francis? Are you in detention?'

'No, Miss Taylor. I'm in choir.'

'You may only be the goalkeeper, Brenda, but we still expect you to turn out for practices. You'll have to explain to Miss Francis that she must manage without you for once. I don't imagine that the choir will collapse if you're missing.'

'No, Miss Taylor.'

'Go on, then. At the double. We'll wait.'

Brenda ran down the steps, aware of the Music Room windows but not looking at them, and back into the corridor. Halfway along it she was halted by a shout from behind.

'*What* do you think you're doing?'

Brenda turned and saw the Head Girl, Gill Rogers, who was also the school hockey captain and had the sense not to try and sing as well.

'Running, Gill. Sorry, Gill.'

'Running's forbidden. You know that. Go back and walk.'

'Miss Taylor told me to run.'

'It's no good trying to blame Miss Taylor; I'm sure she didn't tell you to run.'

'She said at the double,' said Brenda.

'That's not the same thing at all. Go back and *walk*.'

Brenda went back and walked.

'Two minutes and fifteen seconds,' said Miss Francis, reaching for the metronome, when Brenda finally got back to the Music Room. 'Sit down quickly, Brenda. Now then – I said sit down, Brenda.'

'Please, Miss Francis – '

A look of dire agony appeared on Miss Francis's face – it could have been wind so soon after lunch – and she held the metronome in a strangler's grip.

'I think you've delayed us long enough, Brenda.'

'Miss Taylor said couldn't you please excuse me from choir just this once as it's such an important match,' said Brenda, improvising rapidly, since Miss Taylor had said nothing of the sort. Miss Francis raised a claw.

'I believe I made myself perfectly clear the first time. Now, sit down, please.'

'But they're all waiting for me.'

'So are we, Brenda. I must remind you that it is not common practice in this school to postpone activities

35

for the sake of Second Year girls. What position do you occupy in the team? First bat?' Miss Francis knew quite well that there are no bats required in a hockey game, but her ignorance suggested that she was above such things.

'Goalkeeper, Miss Francis.'

'Goalkeeper? From the fuss certain persons are making, I imagined that you must be at least a fast bowler. Is there no one else in the lower school to rival your undoubted excellence at keeping goal?'

'I *did* get chosen for the team, Miss Francis.'

'Clearly you have no equal, Brenda. That being the case, you hardly need to practise, do you?'

'Miss Taylor thinks I do,' said Brenda.

'Well, I'm afraid I don't. I would never, for one moment, keep you from a match, my dear, but a practice on a *Thursday* is an entirely different matter. Sit down.'

Brenda, panicking, pointed to the window. 'But she won't start without me.'

'Neither will I. You may return very quickly and tell Miss Taylor so. At once.'

Brenda set off along the corridor, expecting to hear the first notes of 'An die Musik' break out behind her. There was only silence. They were still waiting.

'Now run and get changed,' said Miss Taylor, swinging her whistle, as Brenda came up the steps again. 'We've waited long enough for you, my girl.'

'Miss Francis says I can't come,' Brenda said, baldly.

'Does she, now?'

'I've got to go back.' A scarcely suppressed jeer rose from the rest of the team, assembled in the Changing Room.

'Brenda, this is the Under-Thirteen Eleven, not the Under-Thirteen Ten. There must be at least sixty of you

in that choir. Are you really telling me that your absence
will be noticed?'

'Miss Francis'll notice it,' said Brenda.

'Then she'll just have to notice it,' said Miss Taylor
under her breath, but loudly enough for Brenda to hear
and appreciate. 'Go and tell Miss Francis that I insist
you attend this practice.'

'Couldn't you give me a note, please?' said Brenda.
Miss Taylor must know that any message sent via
Brenda would be heavily edited before it reached its
destination. She could be as insulting as she pleased in
a note.

'A note?' Brenda might have suggested a dozen red
roses thrown in with it. 'I don't see any reason to send a
note. Simply tell Miss Francis that on this occasion she
must let you go.'

Brenda knew that it was impossible to tell Miss
Francis that she must do anything, and Miss Taylor
knew it too. Brenda put in a final plea for mercy.

'Couldn't you tell her?'

'We've already wasted ten minutes, Brenda, while
you make up your mind.'

'You needn't wait – '

'When I field a team, I field a team, not ten-elevenths
of a team.' She turned and addressed the said team. 'It
seems we'll have to stay here a little longer,' her eyes
strayed to the Music Room windows, 'while Brenda
arrives at her momentous decision.'

Brenda turned and went down the steps again.

'Hurry UP, girl.'

Miss Taylor's huge voice echoed dreadfully round the
confining walls. She should have been in the choir herself, singing bass to Miss Humphry's tenor. Brenda began to run, and like a cuckoo from a clock, Gill Rogers
sprang out of the cloakroom as she cantered past.

'Is that you again?'

Brenda side-stepped briskly and fled towards the Music Room, where she was met by the same ominous silence that had seen her off. The choir, cowed and bowed, crouched over the open music sheets and before them, wearing for some reason her *indomitable* expression, sat Miss Francis, tense as an overwound clockwork mouse and ready for action.

'At last. Really, Brenda, the suspense may prove too much for me. I thought you were never coming back.' She lifted her hands and brought them down sharply on the keys. The choir jerked to attention. An over-eager soprano chimed in and then subsided as Miss Francis raised her hands again and looked round. Brenda was still standing in the doorway.

'Please sit down, Brenda.'

Brenda clung to the door-post and looked hopelessly at Miss Francis. She would have gone down on her knees if there had been the slightest chance that Miss Francis would be moved.

'Well?'

'Please, Miss Francis, Miss Taylor says I *must* go to the practice.' She wished devoutly that she were at home where, should rage break out on this scale, someone would have thrown something. If only Miss Francis would throw something; the metronome, perhaps, through the window.

Tock . . . tock . . . tock . . . *CRASH*! Tinkle tinkle.

But Miss Francis was a lady. With tight restraint she closed the lid of the piano.

'It seems,' she said, in a bitter little voice, 'that we are to have no music today. A hockey game is to take precedence over a choir practice.'

'It's *not* a game,' said Brenda. 'It's a practice, for a

match. Just this once . . .?' she said, and was disgusted to find a tear boiling up under her eyelid. 'Please, Miss Francis.'

'No, Brenda. I do not know why we are enduring this ridiculous debate (Neither do I, Miss Francis) but I thought I had made myself quite clear the first time you asked. You will not miss a scheduled choir practice for an unscheduled hockey practice. Did you not explain to Miss Taylor?'

'Yes I did!' Brenda cried. 'And she said you wouldn't miss me.'

Miss Francis turned all reasonable. 'Miss you? But my dear child, of course we wouldn't miss you. No one would miss you. You are not altogether indispensable, are you?'

'No, Miss Francis.'

'It's a matter of principle. I would not dream of abstracting a girl from a hockey team, or a netball team or even, heaven preserve us, from a shove-ha'penny team, and by the same token I will not allow other members of staff to disrupt my choir practices. Is that clear?'

'Yes, Miss Francis.'

'Go and tell Miss Taylor. I'm sure she'll see my point.'

'Yes, Miss Francis.' Brenda turned to leave, praying that the practice would at last begin without her, but the lid of the piano remained shut.

This time the Head Girl was waiting for her and had her head round the cloakroom door before Brenda was fairly on her way down the corridor.

'Why didn't you come back when I called you, just now?'

Brenda leaned against the wall and let the tear escape, followed by two or three others.

'Are you crying because you've broken rules,' Gill

demanded, 'or because you got caught? I'll see you outside the Sixth-Form Room at four o'clock.'

'It's not my fault.'

'Of course it's your fault. No one forced you to run.'

'They're making me,' said Brenda, pointing two-handed in either direction, towards the Music Room and the Changing Room.

'I daresay you asked for it,' said Gill. 'Four o'clock, please,' and she went back into the Senior cloakroom in the hope of catching some malefactor fiddling with the locks on the lavatory doors.

This last injustice gave Brenda a jolt that she might otherwise have missed, and the tears of self-pity turned hot with anger. She trudged along to the Changing Room.

'You don't exactly hurry yourself, do you?' said Miss Taylor. 'Well?'

'Miss Francis says I can't come to hockey, Miss Taylor.'

Miss Taylor looked round at the restive members of the Under-Thirteen XI and knew that for the good of the game it was time to make a stand.

'Very well, Brenda, I must leave it to you to make up your mind. Either you turn out now for the practice or you forfeit your place in the team. Which is it to be?'

Brenda looked at Miss Taylor, at the Music Room windows, and back to Miss Taylor.

'If I leave now, can I join again later?'

'Good Lord. Is there no end to this girl's cheek? Certainly not. This is your last chance, Brenda.'

It would have to be the choir. She could not bear to hear the singing and never again be part of it, Thursday after Monday, term after term. If you missed a choir practice without permission, you were ejected from the choir. There was no appeal. There would be no permission.

'I'll leave the team, Miss Taylor.'

She saw at once that Miss Taylor had not been expecting this. Her healthy face turned an alarming colour, like Lifebuoy kitchen soap.

'Then there's nothing more to say, is there? This will go on your report, you understand. I cannot be bothered with people who don't take things seriously.'

She turned her back on Brenda and blew the whistle at last, releasing the pent-up team from the Changing Room. They were followed, Brenda noticed, by Pat Stevens, the reserve, who had prudently put on the shin-pads in advance.

Brenda returned to the Music Room. The lid of the piano was still down and Miss Francis's brittle elbow pinned it.

'The prodigal returns,' she announced to the choir as Brenda entered, having seen her approach down the corridor. 'It is now one fifteen. May we begin dear?'

'Yes, Miss Francis.'

'You finally persuaded Miss Taylor to see reason?'

'I told her what you said.'

'And?'

'She said I could choose between missing the choir practice and leaving the team.'

Miss Francis was transformed into an angular little effigy of triumph.

'I see you chose wisely, Brenda.'

'Miss Francis?'

'By coming back to the choir.'

'No, Miss Francis . . .' Brenda began to move towards the door, not trusting herself to come any closer to the piano. 'I'm going to miss choir practice. I came back to tell you.'

'Then you will leave the choir, Brenda. I hope you understand that.'

'Yes, Miss Francis.'

She stepped out of the room for the last time and closed the door. After a long while she heard the first notes of the piano, and the choir finally began to sing. Above the muted voices a whistle shrilled, out on the playing-field. Brenda went and sat in the Junior cloakroom, which was forbidden in lunch hour, and cried. There was no rule against that.

4 How Anthony Made a Friend

'We're lucky to get on so well with the people next door,' said Mr and Mrs Clayton. 'Especially after the last lot.'

The last lot had pushed their piano against the party wall and played a tune called 'Friends and Neighbours' at one o'clock in the morning.

'Do you think they're trying to tell us something?' said Mr Clayton, on the seventh or eighth occasion. Mrs Clayton screamed quietly.

'Playing a tune called "Friends and Neighbours" doesn't qualify them as either, in my opinion,' said Mr Clayton, but quite soon afterwards the owners of the piano moved out, taking their instrument with them, and the Faulkeners moved in.

Mrs Clayton, watching from the landing window, observed that Mr Faulkener was carrying a double-bass, and hurried down to invite Mrs Faulkener in for a cup of tea. Over the cup of tea she casually mentioned the last occupants and the piano. Mrs Faulkener was quick on the uptake.

'Oh, don't worry about us. We go to bed early,' she said.

'They seem a very pleasant couple,' said Mrs Clayton, at tea-time. 'And they have a little girl, about Anthony's age. She'll be company for Anthony, perhaps.'

'Perhaps,' said Mr Clayton.

'Her name's Jenny,' said Mrs Clayton. 'She's staying with her aunt at the moment, but she'll be here on

Saturday. Perhaps Anthony could invite her round for tea.'

'Perhaps,' said Mr Clayton, and made himself busy with the evening paper.

'Would you like that, Anthony?' said Mrs Clayton.

'No,' said Anthony. He sat at the end of the table, tearing holes in a slice of bread and butter. Anyone who did not know that he lived there might have been forgiven for thinking that he had drifted in through the keyhole in a cloud of black smoke. He was thin and dark with little eyes like cold cinders. His hair curled up at the front in horns. At school he prowled round the playground by himself, muttering; to himself. When he came home his mother gave him his tea and sent him out to play with his friends in the street, under the impression that he had some friends to play with. He did not. His favourite person was Anthony Clayton, and he had no time for anyone else. He was nine. He looked thirty, but stunted.

Jenny Faulkener arrived on Saturday, as threatened. She was remarkably like her father's double-bass from the neck down, and her hair was plaited into long gingery pigtails.

'Go and ask her to tea,' said Mrs Clayton, when Anthony showed signs of disappearing into the cupboard under the stairs.

'I'm playing chess,' said Anthony, oozing out again.

'You can't play chess by yourself,' said his mother.

'*I* can,' said Anthony. 'And I'm cheating.'

'Don't be silly,' said his mother. 'Go at once and ask Jenny to tea. They're expecting you.'

Anthony went out of his front gate, turned sharp left and in at the Faulkeners' gate. Jenny opened the door before he had taken his finger off the bell-push. They certainly were expecting him.

'I've got to ask you to tea,' said Anthony.

'That's right,' said Jenny Faulkener. 'I'm all ready.' She stepped out of the house and closed the door behind her.

'You're not coming now, are you?' said Anthony.

'Why not? It's four o'clock.'

'Aren't you going to wash, or anything?'

'You're very rude, aren't you?' said Jenny, as they negotiated the gates. 'My mother said you were a funny little thing.'

'My mother,' said Anthony, '*didn't* say you were a fat lump; but you are.'

'I shall go home if you talk like that,' said Jenny.

'I don't mind,' said Anthony, and opened the gate again, so that she could, but Jenny didn't move.

'It's no good trying to get rid of me,' she said, pityingly. 'Mummy said that you're only peculiar because you're lonely. We're going to be friends.'

'We'll hell as like,' said Anthony, but quietly, because his mother was opening the door.

'You must be Jenny,' she said. 'Come in, dear. We're so pleased you've come to live next door to us. Anthony, take Jenny upstairs to play until tea's ready.'

'I told you it was too early,' said Anthony, as they went up.

Anthony's bedroom was painted pale blue. There was a frilly lampshade hanging from the ceiling and little Donald Ducks on the white window curtains. By the bed lay a fluffy rug with a pussy-cat worked on it.

'Oh, what a lovely room,' cried Jenny, skipping in the sunshine, but then Anthony came in behind her and immediately shadows began to gather in the corners.

'What's that hanging on the bedpost?' said Jenny.

'My noose,' said Anthony.

'Are these your books?'

'They're my mother's books,' said Anthony. 'She buys them for me. These are mine.' He turned his back on the row of new and obviously unopened books and pulled out a drawer at the bottom of the wardrobe. Jenny saw squat volumes bound in crumbling black leather. A smell of old libraries hung about them, of librarians dead and gone.

'What are they about?'

'I don't know,' said Anthony. 'They're all in Latin. I get them off a stall in the market; sixpence each.'

'Why buy them if you can't understand what they say?'

'I like the look of them,' said Anthony.

Jenny looked at him. She could believe it.

'Does your mother always call you Anthony?'

'Yes.'

'Doesn't anyone ever call you Tony?'

'No,' said Anthony.

'I shall.'

'No you won't.'

'You can't stop me.'

'I shan't take any notice, so you can save your breath,' said Anthony, savagely.

'My name's Jennifer, but everyone calls me Jenny, except Auntie May. Auntie calls me Angel-face. I'm not going to call you Anthony.'

'You're not going to call me Angel-face either,' said Anthony, twirling his noose.

'I'll call you An*th*ony,' said Jenny. 'That's how it's spelt.'

Anthony looked daunted for once. 'You can't do that. It sounds silly.'

'Yes, it does,' Jenny agreed. 'But you shouldn't have an "h" in it if you don't want people to say it.'

Mrs Clayton poked a winsome smile round the door.

'Tea-time, children.'

'Ooh, lovely,' said Jenny, with a smile every bit as winsome. 'Come along, Anthony.' She grabbed him by the wrist and yanked him out of the bedroom. She was horribly strong.

'She seems a very sweet child,' said Mrs Clayton, watching Jenny drag Anthony down the street next day. 'I think she'll bring him out of himself.'

'Is that a good thing?' said Mr Clayton. 'Remember Pandora's box.'

Anthony, had he been present, would have agreed with his father. He had barely reached the front gate that morning, when the Faulkeners' window went up with a crash and Jenny leaned out, carolling, 'Anthoneeee! Wait for meeee!'

He had run, but she ran faster.

'Let's play mothers and fathers,' said Jenny.

'Let's play hangman,' said Anthony. 'I'll be the hangman.' He was beginning to realize that having friends might be a good thing after all. There was safety in numbers.

'Are you adopted?' said Jenny.

'What do you mean?'

'Mummy said you might be, because you're so dark and your parents are so fair.'

'I'm a throwback,' Anthony growled. Jenny did not know what he meant, but if such things existed Anthony was definitely one. Someone should throw him back immediately.

'I think you're a changeling,' she confided. 'I think the fairies stole the real Clayton baby and left you in its place.'

'I think you're a fat loony,' said Anthony.

Fortunately Jenny went to a different school, but as

soon as she arrived home, five minutes after he did, she appeared at the door, or scrambled over the back fence. 'Anthony!'

'Glutton for punishment,' said Mr Clayton.

'I think Anthony likes her really, but he's too shy to show it,' said Mrs Clayton.

'Shy?' said her husband. 'If he's shy, I'm King Kong. Why don't you face facts?'

Winter drew near, Anthony's favourite season, when trees shivered naked in the fog and the wind howled across the roofing slates. This year was better still, for on murky evenings Mr Faulkener's bull fiddle could be heard lowing like a damned soul in the distance. But so could his daughter.

'Anthony!'

'Now what?'

'Are you going to make a guy?'

'What for?'

'I'd have thought you'd enjoy burning it,' said Jenny. 'Are you having fireworks?'

'I don't like fireworks,' said Anthony, forbearing to add that his mother did not like them either.

'Oh well, you can watch ours. We have a firework party every year and invite all our friends. You can come – '

'I don't *like* fireworks.'

'You're my friend. We'll make the guy together.'

Mrs Clayton did not really approve of making guys, but she did so like to see Jenny and Anthony side by side, the golden head and the dark one. She rarely troubled to overhear what the dark head had to say to the golden head, which was possibly just as well.

'I bet you've got nits in your pigtails, Codface,' said Anthony.

A pyre began to rise in the Faulkeners' garden; tier

upon tier of crushed tea-chests, brushwood, off-cuts and old chair-legs. Anthony provided the chair-legs.

'Wherever did you get so many old chair-legs, dear?' said Mrs Faulkener.

'Off old chairs,' said Anthony, with a scowl that made Mrs Faulkener want to scurry indoors to see how her furniture was getting along.

Mrs Faulkener and Mrs Clayton each contributed a pile of cast-off clothes to make the guy. Jenny assembled it and Anthony watched. It grew. It swelled. It developed into an elegant creature with a wasp waist and a stunning bosom full of old stockings. Jenny made its head out of a pillow case and painted a face on it with blank, long-lashed eyes, rosy cheeks and a cupid's-bow mouth. It sat in a chair and simpered, while Jenny stitched a pink felt hat on its head, trimmed with pigeon feathers.

'It's a lady guy,' said Jenny. 'I'm going to call it Guyella.'

'It looks like you,' said Anthony.

'Have you seen the children's guy?' said Mrs Faulkener to Mrs Clayton. Anthony realized that he was being held jointly responsible for the monstrous dolly, and saw his reputation in ruins. There were still some old clothes left over and he set about constructing a rival. Jenny, reasonably enough, had taken the best garments for the first guy, but there remained a bolster case, a pair of black woollen stockings and a sweater or two. Anthony borrowed a needle from his mother and went to work. Next morning Mrs Clayton nearly found an early grave when she discovered Anthony's guy lying across the end of his bed in the cold November light.

Anthony's guy was nine feet long. It had four arms and a pointed head. Its chin was gathered into its neck so that it looked as if it were being strangled, and

Anthony had sewn its legs on back to front so that its black woolly toes pointed perversely in the opposite direction from its face.

Anthony came down to breakfast with the guy slung over his shoulder like a fireman rescuing a victim, although it was difficult to imagine Anthony rescuing anyone. After the table was cleared Anthony conducted his guy to the front gate, dragging it by one leg, for maximum effect. In the adjoining gateway Jenny had set up Guyella in an old push-chair, and she was explaining to a neighbour that she and Anthony had made it together.

'I hope you are not asking for pennies,' said the neighbour. 'I always think that that is a kind of begging.'

'Oh no,' said Jenny, 'but it's such a lovely guy, we wanted everyone to see it.'

'It's too pretty to burn,' said the neighbour, and then let out a dismayed squeak, for looking over Jenny's head she had seen Anthony emerging followed, inch by inch, by his guy.

'Ooh, An*th*ony's made one, too,' cried Jenny. Wordlessly, Anthony hoisted his creature to its feet and draped its spineless carcass over the gatepost so that it leered down at Guyella with a speculative eye; one speculative eye.

'Good God,' said the neighbour, faintly.

'This is Flabber,' said Anthony, deftly arranging the four arms so that the guy had every appearance of swarming up the gatepost and doing something unspeakable on the other side.

'Oh, An*th*ony,' said Jenny. 'It's horrid.'

'I should move Guyella, if I was you,' said Anthony, 'before it gets over.'

Anthony, who had never been one for teddy-bears and gollywogs, became decidedly attached to Flabber. It slept, coiled like a boa constrictor, on the end of his bed, and accompanied him to meals, where it sat slumped on its own chair at the corner of the table.

'Does that revolting thing have to eat with us?' demanded Anthony's father, flicking one of Flabber's four hands away from the cake-plate.

'Sssh, dear. Anthony's so fond of it,' said Mrs Clayton.

'That figures,' said Mr Clayton.

Mrs Faulkener did not care for Flabber either. 'Perhaps you'd like to leave it in the garden?' she suggested, when Anthony came round to play, with his invertebrate chum lagging his narrow neck.

'It will get cold, poor sweet,' said Anthony, in a voice

that was suspiciously similar to Jenny's. He went upstairs and Flabber slithered behind, its pointed head knocking softly on each step.

All the same, it was Guyella who attracted the praise and attention. People stopped to admire Guyella, and if they admired Flabber, they preferred not to mention it. Also, Jenny with her golden plaits was more approachable than swart and surly Anthony.

'That thing gives me the creeps,' Mr Faulkener complained, after a high wind dislodged Flabber and he found it lying across his gateway.

'Never mind,' said Mrs Faulkener. 'They'll be burning it on Friday.'

'But not little Anthony, alas,' said Mr Faulkener, and Mrs Faulkener was deeply shocked, because her husband was a kindly man and loved children.

Anthony, as it happened, was at that moment leaning over the bannisters.

Next morning, Flabber and Guyella were put out to take the air as usual, but quite early on Jenny was sent to the corner shop to buy biscuits for elevenses. When she returned, Guyella had gone.

Jenny wept. 'Why didn't you keep an eye on them?' she demanded, when Anthony came out to see what the keening was about.

'I was busy,' Anthony said. 'What a good thing Flabber wasn't stolen as well;' for Flabber was still clinging like a squid to the gatepost. It looked smug, almost sleek, on account of its fortunate escape. One might have imagined that it had put on weight. It had hips, where no hips had been before.

Inquiries were made up and down the street, but no one had been seen abducting Guyella. 'I expect it was those boys from down the Lane,' was the best help anyone could give.

'Well, darling, you've still got Anthony's er – guy,' said Mrs Faulkener.

'I wish they'd pinched that instead,' said Jenny.

'Don't be selfish,' said her mother, who was thinking the same thing. 'And don't say "pinched". It sounds so common.'

November the Fifth arrived, but Guyella did not come home. Jenny was consoled with boxes of fireworks, and went round to remind Anthony that the party started at seven.

'Shall I take Flabber now, An*th*ony? So that Daddy can put him on the bonfire?'

'No,' said Anthony. 'He's coming with me.'

'But he ought to be up there ready when the party starts.'

'Then I'll come early,' said Anthony.

Mr and Mrs Clayton and Anthony and Flabber arrived early, as promised, but so did all the other guests, who were mostly friends and neighbours from the Faulkeners' old home: so there was a fair-sized crowd assembled with torches when the great row took place. Some of the friends and neighbours looked taken aback when Flabber loomed out of the darkness, suspended from Mrs Clayton's clothes prop. Mr Faulkener put on his gardening gloves and squared up to Flabber with tremendous good humour.

'Right, my lad. Up you go.'

Anthony jerked the clothes prop. Flabber curtsied and receded into the night.

'We've only come to watch,' said Anthony.

'I understood we were going to burn it,' said Mr Faulkener, his good humour slipping a little.

'Don't be silly, dear,' said Mrs Clayton.

'No! No! I don't want it burned,' Anthony yelled,

swinging the prop wildly so that Flabber sashayed in and out of the torch light.

'Well, we're going to burn it, Anthony Clayton, so there!' Jenny shouted, and darting foward she seized Flabber by its retrograde feet. Simultaneously, Anthony dropped the clothes prop and flung his arms round Flabber's chest. They both dug their heels in and tugged. The grown-ups tutted and shuffled, and one voice in the dark muttered, 'Oh, that *awful* child.' Mrs Clayton hoped it meant Jenny. Everyone else assumed it meant Anthony.

Jenny and Anthony meanwhile, teeth clenched, surged back and forth with Flabber horribly stretched out taut between them. Suddenly there was a loud ripping sound and certain vital threads gave way. Jenny sat down hard with Flabber's legs in her lap, while Anthony rolled over backwards, clutching the major remains of Flabber. From Flabber's martyred body slid Guyella, head first and still smirking. There was a nasty silence until Mrs Clayton cried, 'Oh, Anthony! That was very naughty of you to steal poor Jenny's guy.'

'You sewed her up in your horrible *thing*!' Jenny wailed.

'I think you should *do* something about that child,' said Mrs Faulkener, but Anthony still lay on the ground with Flabber on top of him. From under the tangled heap came a strange sound that no one had ever heard before. Anthony was laughing.

'Get up at once!' roared his father, but it was all Anthony could do to sit. Still giggling, he pointed a shaking finger at Flabber's other end and shrieked, '*It's having a baby*!'

Anthony was not allowed to stay for the firework

party. With Flabber's short corpse tucked under his arm, he was sent home in disgrace, and told to go straight to bed, which he did. For the first time in his life he fell asleep with a smile on his face.

5 Marrow Hill

All the Burton children looked barmy. They had mad gleeful faces and wild weak eyes behind thick glasses, through which they ogled like loony goldfish. They all wore glasses. There seemed to be ten of them, twenty swivelling eyes, but it was possible to count them when they stopped moving and there were only four after all; eight eyes.

I saw the Burtons once a year, when I went to stay with my Aunt Eileen for two weeks, in the summer holidays. Aunt Eileen lived in a street that was just like our street, in a town that was just like ours. The only thing that turned the visit into a holiday was the hour-long journey there by bus. Once I got off the bus, everything was much the same as it was at home, except for the Burtons.

The Burtons lived next door to Aunt Eileen. All the other back gardens in the street had palings round them, no more than waist height, but the Burtons were surrounded by a tall corrugated iron fence with woundy-looking spikes on top.

'To stop them getting out,' said Aunt Eileen, who lived next door to them all the year round. In the front garden the Burtons' privet hedge grew high and secretive, screening the bay window where the blinds were always down. After I had been staying with Aunt Eileen for three consecutive summers, I knew all the neighbours in her row, but none of them knew the Burtons. They were like a rare and unpredictable species in a cage at the zoo; you looked, but you didn't poke your fingers through the bars.

I did my looking from an upstairs window. If I went into the bathroom and stood on the Lloyd Loom laundry-basket, I could see over the corrugated iron fence into the Burtons' garden, and almost into their back room, through the french windows. Even when the windows were open the curtains were drawn, but sometimes, when a Burton came out, I got a glimpse of a bamboo table and a hairy rug like a dead dog that had been shot down on the threshold while defending its master.

By leaning far out I could see right down to the end of the Burtons' garden. They had an ash tree in the corner and the grass grew long like meadow grass. I suppose that it had been a lawn once, because there was a dent in the middle that might have been a flowerbed. The iron fence was overgrown with blackberry vines that straggled across to our side in places, although the berries were never black when I was there.

One summer the Burtons had a tent. We had a tent at home, which my father put up for us when we could persuade him, but the Burtons erected their own. They tried to. Eldest Burton stood in the middle and gave orders while the other three, or nine, milled round him with guy-lines and tent-pegs and a mallet with which they crushed their own and each others' fingers.

The two middle Burtons were girls. They jumped up and down a lot, shrieking: 'Oh, I say! What shall I do with this? Oh, I say! What have you done with that? Oh, get out of the way, you ass. You drip. You clot. You wet. You utter *weed*! Oh! Oh! Oh!'

'Oh, shut up!' yelled Eldest Burton, laying about him with the ridge-pole.

'Oh, don't be beastly, Specs,' the others screamed, and threw themselves down to roll in the long grass, waving their legs in the air and braying.

I thought they had a nerve, calling him Specs, because as I said, they all wore glasses. If he had a proper name, they never used it, and he never used theirs. They called each other Specs, Tiddy, Bunny, Twizzle and Smudge, quite arbitrarily. He who was Smudge one day might be Twizzle the next. I could never tell which was which, and when they lost their tempers they were all drips, clots, asses, wets and utter weeds.

Even their mother didn't seem to know their names. When she wanted them she stood at the top of the steps by the back door and called them collectively: 'Darleeengs!' and they would drop whatever they were doing, usually each other, and swarm up the garden like lemmings, breathless and still yelling.

'What, Mummy, what, Mummy; Mummy, Mummy, what?'

Some days they played cricket. They always began very seriously, setting up stumps and excavating a crease in the jungle vegetation. The bowler had to begin his run inside the back room, burst through the french windows, down the steps and let go the ball at the top of the rockery, which was overgrown to the point where it looked like the foothills of the Himalaya. This delivery was followed by a reverberant clang as the ball hit the iron fence, for the Burtons' cricket season was one long succession of maiden overs – except once. Once Youngest Burton kept his bat down and hit a six. I saw the ball descend among Aunt Eileen's tomato plants.

I leaped off the linen basket, ran downstairs and out into the garden. I couldn't believe my luck – at last, a chance to meet them. We might talk. I reached the garden path. I stopped.

There was a Burton in Aunt Eileen's tomatoes.

It was Elder Middle Burton. Younger Middle Burton

and Youngest Burton were astride the iron fence, in horrid danger of being impaled on the spikes.

'Do you want your ball?' I said, coldly.

Elder Middle Burton sprang out of the tomatoes, whooping like a klaxon with laughter, or simple insanity, and went up the fence the way a cat goes up curtains. All three Burtons vanished simultaneously and I heard them recounting their adventures to Eldest.

'Oh! Oh! I say! Specs . . . in the garden . . . oh! There's – a – funny – little – girl!'

That was me.

'I'm not half as funny as you are!' I yelled, and went indoors, hating them. But I was soon back on the laundry basket.

Aunt Eileen let me sleep in her big front bedroom, in the big swampy double bed that she had once shared with my uncle. His name had been Percy, but he had died before I knew him, and I always thought of him as Uncle Eileen. From the window in that room I could watch Father and Mother Burton set off on evening excursions.

Father would come out first, jangling keys as though he were about to leap into a powerful car and roar away. I don't think they had a car at all; he went to work on a sit-up-and-beg push-bike. Then Mother Burton floated down the path, all draped in white like a night-scented flower that attracts moths. She would stand at the gate, keening farewells to the mob who hung out of the windows – surely there were ten of them at night – rattling the wooden slats of the venetian blinds like castanets, while her thin high voice spiralled eerily above the yoiks and tally-hoes of her offspring.

'Good-bye, my darleeengs. Take care of each other for Mummy. Good-byeee!'

'You would think,' said Aunt Eileen, peering over my shoulder, 'that they were going to the opera.'

Mother and Father Burton moved off; he sub-fusc and already lost in the shadows, she catching the last of the sunset and glimmering up the road.

'Where are they going, then?' I said, as the Burtons slammed down every single front window, one after the other. These thuds were followed by a dislocated clatter as the venetian blinds descended.

'To the Odeon, probably,' said Aunt Eileen. 'There's a good film on, this week. Shall we go, tomorrow?'

I lay in bed, looking forward to that, and listening to the thumps and crashes next door, which was the Burtons taking care of each other for Mummy.

A few days later they got hold of a camera. It was a square black box with bits sticking out of the sides, and it looked like a device for detonating gelignite. The camera seemed to be common property, like their clothes which appeared indiscriminately on each Burton in turn, and they fought savagely over it, while carrying on the usual conversation.

'Oh! Filthy pig! *My* turn. Bags I next. Rotten beast!' Knuckles rang against teeth. 'Utter weed! *My* turn. Oh! Ouch! Leggo!'

'Yarroo,' murmured Aunt Eileen, passing by with clean towels.

Sometime towards the middle of the afternoon, one of the Burtons actually got its hands on the camera for long enough to make the others line up and be photographed. They draped their arms round each other and smiled with lolling heads, so that they looked as if they had all been garrotted. For once I felt as though I shouldn't be looking, as though I had witnessed something that ordinary people shouldn't see.

It was the strangest sight. They seemed to be pretending to be children so that they could display the photograph and say, 'Look. This proves it. We're real.' But they didn't look real, and the longer they stood there, the less real they looked; not only pretending to be children, but pretending to be alive. After the shutter had clicked there was another fight and the camera was flung into the rockery where it fell against a stone and burst open. At that moment, Mother Burton began her banshee routine at the top of the steps and they all thundered indoors. I fetched Uncle Eileen's army field-glasses and took a closer look at the camera. There was no film in it.

I was almost convinced then that the Burtons were ghosts, and not children's ghosts: grown-up ghosts doing all the things that they thought children should do. But next day Youngest Burton cut his chin on the door-scraper while biting his sister in the leg, and bled real blood, so that theory was no good. All the same, I began to watch to see if they had shadows. It was hard to tell, they moved so fast. I decided that they had only one shadow between them, like the weird sisters with their single eye.

That was the year they got the tortoise.

I knew from the start that they had made a grave mistake with that tortoise. It was the wrong pet. When it arrived they put it down in the grass and danced round it, singing a tortoise-warming song. They called it Flash, which was supposed to be a joke, I think. They treated it as one of themselves, pushing it about like a toy tank and howling encouragement but, wisely, it wouldn't come out. I imagine that they hoped to train it to jump through hoops and fetch sticks, and I wondered what would happen when they discovered that it wouldn't cooperate; but before it could be persuaded to join them at cricket, it got under the iron fence and went to live three doors down with the Rodgerses, who knew when to keep their mouths shut.

They tried again the following year, and this time they got it right. They got a dog and it was the right kind of dog, curly-tailed and hysterical. It was a proper children's-book dog; they called it Sammy, which was the right kind of name, and it behaved in the right kind of way, woofing and barking, leaping off the ground on all four legs at once and looking up at the Burtons with intelligent doggy eyes when they told it secrets.

'Oh! *Angel*-Sammy. He understands *everything* we say,' they bawled at each other. Most of the time, though, they bawled at the dog.

'Fetch Sammy! Catch, Sammy! Beg, Sammy! Die for the King, Sammy!' The King was already dead, but Sammy lay down anyway, dead as the hairy rug by the french windows. I wondered if they had text books: *How to be a Child*: *How to be a Child with a Dog*. Sammy clearly had one too: *How to be a Children's Dog*.

There was so much riot in the Burtons' garden that it was several days before I noticed that one Burton was missing, and a little longer before I realized that it was always the same one. From time to time Eldest Burton would disappear. I never saw him go or come back, and for a while I supposed that he was dematerializing behind the ash tree.

The Burtons had a back gate, but they didn't go through it, any more than they went through the front gate. They were contained. Aunt Eileen had a back gate too, opening on to the mud path along the ends of the gardens, and on the other side of the path were allotments. One day I went through our gate just as Eldest Burton was climbing over his. I drew back into the garden until he was well clear, and then followed at a canny distance. A Burton on the loose: was society at risk?

Eldest Burton went under a bulge in the chain-link fence and made off into the plantation of pea-sticks and bean rows, through a froth of cauliflowers and behind the raspberry-canes. Now, there was a wasted opportunity. It occured to me that if the Burtons hoped to pass for real children, they ought to be out raiding the allotments every day, but possibly they had not yet reached the chapter on scrumping in the text book. Eldest Burton kept going until he got to the place where the ground fell away towards the flour mill and the river. There was an old Nissen hut here, and I crept round it, keeping my head well down behind the nettles and fat hen plants. I rather hoped to catch him changing back into whatever he was really – not a child – but when I reached the end of the Nissen hut, he was just sitting still with his back to me. He was sitting on a mound of earth surrounded by vegetable marrows.

I trod on an old cloche that broke up with a crunch, and he looked round.

'What do you want?' he said. That was all he said, and he just said it, in an ordinary voice, like people did who weren't Burtons. I was so surprised, I couldn't think of a lie.

'I was following you,' I said.

'You live next door, don't you?' he said.

'Sometimes. I stay with my Aunt Eileen in the summer holidays.'

This was the cue for him to bounce up on end and shriek, 'Hooray for the Hols!' which was exactly what he would have done in his own back garden, but he didn't.

'I thought I didn't see you very often,' he said.

I thought that this was putting it mildly. Where did he imagine I got to during the other fifty weeks of the year?

65

'Are you going to make a row?' he said.

'No.'

'Then welcome to Marrow Hill. Come on up.'

I went on up, between the marrow plants, and sat down beside him at the top. There was a kind of flat hard place to sit on. I guessed that he must have worn it smooth and that he came here often.

'Are these your marrows?'

'No.'

'Your dad's, I mean.'

'He doesn't grow things.'

I thought of the garden behind the iron fence. 'No.'

'He grew a nasturtium, once.'

'What happened to it?'

'He killed it,' said Eldest Burton, and I imagined Father Burton with a shotgun, waiting behind the hedge for the nasturtium to come round the corner. 'It took so long to come up, he forgot what it was. He thought it was a weed.'

'Well, whose marrows are they?'

'I don't know,' he said. 'It doesn't matter. I don't do them any harm. They know me.' I wasn't sure that I had heard him aright. 'Look at this one.' He patted the largest marrow of all. 'This is old man Grimshaw.'

'*Who*?'

'Old Grimshaw; he's the gaffer. I knew him when he was that long.' Eldest Burton indicated something the size of a chipolata sausage between thumb and forefinger. 'And this is Adelaide Bulk. That's Henry the Eighth and here – ' he moved some leaves and uncovered a welter-weight and a runt, ' – are Laurel and Hardy. Look behind you.'

I looked. There crouched a marrow so variously striped that it seemed to be stuffed into a tartan skin.

'Wee Hamish McBagpipe.'

He introduced me to every marrow on the mound, right down to the Babe-in-Arms who was one inch long and still had a flower on the end. It turned out that the marrows were all related; all descended from Gaffer Grimshaw, and Eldest Burton kindly explained who was whose father, aunt, cousin, nephew. I noticed that there didn't seem to be any brothers or sisters among them. Then he sat back, resting on his elbows, and whistled quietly. He whistled 'Christians, Awake', which was an odd choice for August as it usually gets sung on Christmas morning. I half expected the marrows to be charmed and rise up on gently swaying stalks.

Perhaps he *was* barmy; not Burton-barmy but plain honest-to-goodness round the bend. Perhaps I should humour him.

'Don't you find them a bit boring?' I asked, looking at his supine friends.

'No.' He seemed surprised. 'Of course they're not boring.'

'But you can't – well, you can't play cricket with marrows, can you?'

'No,' he agreed happily. 'You can't.'

'And they don't talk to you, do they?'

'No.'

'What do they do, then?' I asked.

'Do?' said Eldest Burton. He smiled blissfully. 'They don't do anything.'

6 William's Version

William and Granny were left to entertain each other for an hour while William's mother went to the clinic.

'Sing to me,' said William.

'Granny's too old to sing,' said Granny.

'I'll sing to you, then,' said William. William only knew one song. He had forgotten the words and the tune, but he sang it several times, anyway.

'Shall we do something else now?' said Granny.

'Tell me a story,' said William. 'Tell me about the wolf.'

'Red Riding Hood?'

'No, not *that* wolf, the other wolf.'

'Peter and the wolf?' said Granny.

'Mummy's going to have a baby,' said William.

'I know,' said Granny.

William looked suspicious.

'How do you know?'

'Well . . . she told me. And it shows, doesn't it?'

'The lady down the road had a baby. It looks like a pig,' said William. He counted on his fingers. 'Three babies looks like three pigs.'

'Ah,' said Granny. 'Once upon a time there were three little pigs. Their names were – '

'They didn't have names,' said William.

'Yes they did. The first pig was called – '

'Pigs don't have names.'

'Some do. These pigs had names.'

'No they didn't.' William slid off Granny's lap and went to open the corner cupboard by the fireplace. Old magazines cascaded out as old magazines do when they have been flung into a cupboard and the door slammed shut. He rooted among them until he found a little book covered with brown paper, climbed into the cupboard, opened the book, closed it and climbed out again. 'They didn't have names,' he said.

'I didn't know you could read,' said Granny, properly impressed.

'C – A – T, wheelbarrow,' said William.

'Is that the book Mummy reads to you out of?'

'It's my book,' said William.

'But it's the one Mummy reads?'

'If she says please,' said William.

'Well, that's Mummy's story, then. My pigs have names.'

'They're the wrong pigs.' William was not open to negotiation. 'I don't want them in this story.'

'Can't we have different pigs this time?'

'No. They won't know what to do.'

'Once upon a time,' said Granny, 'there were three little pigs who lived with their mother.'

'Their mother was dead,' said William.

'Oh, I'm sure she wasn't,' said Granny.

'She was dead. You make bacon out of dead pigs. She got eaten for breakfast and they threw the rind out for the birds.'

'So the three little pigs had to find homes for themselves.'

'No.' William consulted his book. 'They had to build little houses.'

'I'm just coming to that.'

'You said they had to *find* homes. They didn't *find* them.'

'The first little pig walked along for a bit until he met a man with a load of hay.'

69

'It was a lady.'

'A lady with a load of hay?'

'NO! It was a lady-pig. You said *he*.'

'I thought all the pigs were little boy-pigs,' said Granny.

'It says lady-pig here,' said William. 'It says the lady-pig went for a walk and met a man with a load of hay.'

'So the lady-pig,' said Granny, 'said to the man, "May I have some of that hay to build a house?" and the man said, "Yes." Is that right?'

'Yes,' said William. 'You know that baby?'

'What baby?'

'The one Mummy's going to have. Will that baby have shoes on when it comes out?'

'I don't think so,' said Granny.

'It will have cold feet,' said William.

'Oh no,' said Granny. 'Mummy will wrap it up in a soft shawl, all snug.'

'I don't *mind* if it has cold feet,' William explained. 'Go on about the lady-pig.'

'So the little lady-pig took the hay and built a little house. Soon the wolf came along and the wolf said – '

'You didn't tell where the wolf lived.'

'I don't know where the wolf lived.'

'15 Tennyson Avenue, next to the bomb-site,' said William.

'I bet it doesn't say that in the book,' said Granny, with spirit.

'Yes it does.'

'Let me see, then.'

William folded himself up with his back to Granny, and pushed the book up under his pullover.

'*I* don't think it says that in the book,' said Granny.

'It's in ever so small words,' said William.

'So the wolf said, "Little pig, little pig, let me come

in,'' and the little pig answered, ''No''. So the wolf said, ''Then I'll huff and I'll puff and I'll blow your house down,'' and he huffed and he puffed and he blew the house down, and the little pig ran away.'

'He ate the little pig,' said William.

'No, no,' said Granny. 'The little pig ran away.'

'He ate the little pig. He ate her in a sandwich.'

'All right, he ate the little pig in a sandwich. So the second little pig – '

'You didn't tell about the tricycle.'

'What about the tricycle?'

'The wolf got on his tricycle and went to the bread shop to buy some bread. To make the sandwich,' William explained, patiently.

'Oh well, the wolf got on his tricycle and went to the bread shop to buy some bread. And he went to the grocer's to buy some butter.' This innovation did not go down well.

'He already had some butter in the cupboard,' said William.

'So then the second little pig went for a walk and met a man with a load of wood, and the little pig said to the man, ''May I have some of that wood to build a house?'' and the man said,''Yes.'' '

'He didn't say please.'

' ''Please may I have some of that wood to build a house?'' '

'It was sticks.'

'Sticks *are* wood.'

William took out his book and turned the pages. 'That's right,' he said.

'Why don't you tell the story?' said Granny.

'I can't remember it,' said William.

'You could read it out of your book.'

'I've lost it,' said William, clutching his pullover.

'Look, do you know who this is?' He pulled a green angora scarf from under the sofa.

'No, who is it?' said Granny, glad of the diversion.

'This is Doctor Snake.' He made the scarf wriggle across the carpet.

'Why is he a doctor?'

'Because he is all furry,' said William. He wrapped the doctor round his neck and sat sucking the loose end. 'Go on about the wolf.'

'So the little pig built a house of sticks and along came the wolf – on his tricycle?'

'He came by bus. He didn't have any money for a ticket so he ate up the conductor.'

'That wasn't very nice of him,' said Granny.

'No,' said William. 'It wasn't *very* nice.'

'And the wolf said, "Little pig, little pig, let me come in," and the little pig said, "No," and the wolf said, "Then I'll huff and I'll puff and I'll blow your house down," so he huffed and he puffed and he blew the house down. And then what did he do?' Granny asked, cautiously.

William was silent.

'Did he eat the second little pig?'

'Yes.'

'How did he eat this little pig?' said Granny, prepared for more pig sandwiches or possibly pig on toast.

'With his mouth,' said William.

'Now the third little pig went for a walk and met a man with a load of bricks. And the little pig said, "*Please* may I have some of those bricks to build a house?" and the man said, "Yes." So the little pig took the bricks and built a house.'

'He built it on the bomb-site.'

'Next door to the wolf?' said Granny. 'That was very silly of him.'

'There wasn't anywhere else,' said William. 'All the roads were full up.'

'The wolf didn't have to come by bus or tricycle this time, then, did he?' said Granny, grown cunning.

'Yes.' William took out the book and peered in, secretively. 'He was playing in the cemetery. He had to get another bus.'

'And did he eat the conductor this time?'

'No. A nice man gave him some money, so he bought a ticket.'

'I'm glad to hear it,' said Granny.

'He ate the nice man,' said William.

'So the wolf got off the bus and went up to the little

73

pig's house, and he said, "Little pig, little pig, let me come in," and the little pig said, "No," and then the wolf said, "I'll huff and I'll puff and I'll blow your house down," and he huffed and he puffed and he huffed and he puffed but he couldn't blow the house down because it was made of bricks.'

'He couldn't blow it down,' said William, 'because it was stuck to the ground.'

'Well, anyway, the wolf got very cross then, and he climbed on the roof and shouted down the chimney, "I'm coming to get you!" but the little pig just laughed and put a big saucepan of water on the fire.'

'He put it on the gas stove.'

'He put it on the *fire*,' said Granny, speaking very rapidly, 'and the wolf fell down the chimney and into the pan of water and was boiled and the little pig ate him for supper.'

William threw himself full length on the carpet and screamed.

'He didn't! He didn't! *He didn't*! He didn't eat the wolf.'

Granny picked him up, all stiff and kicking, and sat him on her lap.

'Did I get it wrong again, love? Don't cry. Tell me what really happened.'

William wept, and wiped his nose on Doctor Snake.

'The little pig put the saucepan on the gas stove and the wolf got down the chimney and put the little pig in the saucepan and boiled him. He had him for tea, with chips,' said William.

'Oh,' said Granny. 'I've got it all wrong, haven't I? Can I see the book, then I shall know, next time.'

William took the book from under his pullover. Granny opened it and read, *First Aid for Beginners: a Practical Handbook*.

'I see,' said Granny. 'I don't think I can read this. I left my glasses at home. You tell Gran how it ends.'

William turned to the last page which showed a prostrate man with his leg in a splint; *compound fracture of the femur*.

'Then the wolf washed up and got on his tricycle and went to see his Granny, and his Granny opened the door and said, "Hello, William." '

'I thought it was the wolf.'

'It was. It was the wolf. His name was William Wolf,' said William.

'What a nice story,' said Granny. 'You tell it much better than I do.'

'I can see up your nose,' said William. 'It's all whiskery.'

7 Divine Melodious Truth

Judith's friend Arthur Kemp was a mine of information. Judith's mum said, Yes, but it was a pity Arthur didn't check his facts more carefully. Judith's dad said that Arthur was a five-star liar with knobs on and flames coming out at the top.

Arthur was of a scientific bent. He liked things with cogs and ratchets and levers that could be twiddled and adjusted. He showed Judith a little metal cylinder with a row of numbers in a window at the side.

'Look,' said Arthur, 'if you turn this bit at the end, all the numbers go round.'

Judith turned the little bit at the end and the numbers went round.

'What's it for?'

'When all the numbers get in a certain order, it will blow up,' said Arthur, twiddling busily.

'What order's that?' said Judith.

'I don't know,' said Arthur. 'I'm trying to find out.' Judith was impressed by Arthur's reckless courage in the interests of science.

'It sounds like the mileometer off a bicycle,' said Judith's dad, when Judith described Arthur's infernal machine. 'I wonder whose bike he got it off.'

'Oh, come now,' said Mum. 'He doesn't pinch things.'

'I suppose not,' said Dad. 'Why should he? He can invent anything he wants, out of thin air.'

Arthur's family had a telephone installed.

'Do you know what happens if you dial your own

number?' said Arthur. 'It jams up the exchange. All the phones in England will stop working.'

'Try it,' said Judith.

'It would be a crime,' said Arthur, piously.

Later he furnished some more information on the subject. 'If lightning struck a telephone pole while you were on the phone, you'd be struck too,' said Arthur. 'Never brush your hair in a thunderstorm. It attracts the lightning.'

'If you mix sugar with soap flakes, it explodes,' he added, by way of a bonus.

'Man will never get to the moon,' said Arthur, 'because it's moving away from us at a million miles a year.'

'Why doesn't it look smaller, then?' said Peter Millum.

'Parallax,' said Arthur.

Sometimes Arthur told the truth, by accident, but Judith and Peter had never caught him at it. Judith always wanted to believe Arthur because, without doubt, Arthur believed passionately in everything that he said; but Peter was a sceptic. Peter had never believed anything since the lady on the corner told him that stars were angels' eyes, shining with tears because little boys and girls on earth were so naughty.

'They are too far apart,' said Peter, who was then five. Now he was eight and useless for playing with, because he kept going home to look things up in the Encyclopaedia, especially when he was playing with Arthur.

'I don't believe you,' he said to Arthur, several times a day.

'I should know,' said Arthur. 'I'm older than you.'

Peter went off to ask Arthur's mother when Arthur was born. She had to fetch Arthur's birth certificate from the middle drawer of the dresser before Peter would go away.

While Peter was at Arthur's house an aeroplane flew over.

'That's the Comet,' said Arthur.

'The Comet's a jet,' said Judith.

'So was that.'

'But I could see the propellers.'

'It was the Comet.'

'But it was too *slow*.'

'It had its brakes on,' said Arthur.

Arthur's family bought a television set.

'My uncle invented television,' said Arthur.

'The television was invented by John Logie Baird,' said Peter, next day, after a prolonged consultation with the Encyclopaedia.

'*And* my uncle,' said Arthur. 'My uncle works for the BBC.'

'Well, that's true – for a wonder,' said Judith's dad. 'He's an electrician at Broadcasting House.'

'Told you,' said Arthur.

On wet days Judith and Peter went up to Arthur's attic to listen to Arthur's gramophone. Arthur's parents had a large wireless cabinet in their living-room, that worked off accumulator batteries. From time to time Arthur's father took the accumulators down to the garage to have them recharged and topped up with distilled water.

'With electricity,' said Arthur.

'How'd they get it in?' said Judith.

'It's compressed,' said Arthur. 'Compressed electricity. They have a pump.'

Arthur himself had an old gramophone that had belonged to his granny before she died (of air on the brain, according to Arthur. 'Just like Arthur,' said

Judith's dad). Arthur treated his gramophone with great care, polishing the wooden case once a week, shining up the brass knobs on the doors at the front, and oiling their hinges. The doors were very important. If you wanted to increase the volume, you opened the doors, wide or ajar, according to taste. This was a great improvement on the gramophone in Judith's house, which had to be stuffed with old vests when it became too noisy.

On one side of the instrument was a handle, like the starting handle on Arthur's father's car, which was used for winding up the motor between records. If one forgot to do this the gramophone would turn faint and grind to a halt, while the music died away with a low moan.

Playing a record on Arthur's gramophone was a matter of some ceremony. Arthur kindly explained what he was doing while he did it. First he raised the lid and propped it open. Then he took a steel needle from the little box by the turntable and screwed it into the socket on the end of the pick-up. The needle had to be changed between records.

'The vibrations from the record travel up the needle into the pick-up,' said Arthur. Peter looked dubious. It sounded almost likely.

'How'd you get music from vibrations?'

'The pick-up picks up radio waves from the air and turns them into sound,' said Arthur. 'That's why it's called a pick-up.' Peter looked more dubious still.

'Choose a record,' said Arthur. 'It's Peter's turn.' Peter had his selection all ready. It was the 'Fairy Song', from *The Immortal Hour*, according to the label. Peter, for some reason, called it the frog song.

'How many grooves on a gramophone record?' said Arthur.

'Four thousand?' Judith guessed.

'Two!' said Arthur, gleefully. 'One on each side.'

'Don't believe you,' said Peter, trying to count. Arthur slapped his hand away.

'Never put your fingers on a record surface,' said Arthur. 'Your fingers are full of grease deposits. The needle will skid. Your turn now, Jude.'

Judith sorted through the pile of discs in their paper sleeves. Arthur's record collection was of the same vintage as Arthur's gramophone. Arthur's granny must have danced to it in her youth. Some of the records had grooves on one side only, and one of them was actually two of these stuck together; called, not surprisingly, The Twin. Several were only a few inches across and had enticing names: 'Shanghai'; 'The Black Bottom'; 'Chilli-bom-bom'. 'Chilli-bom-bom' had a crack in it. Round it went.

'*I – love – my – Chilli – bom – bom – bom – bom – bom – bom . . .*'

'What's the Black Bottom?' said Peter. 'It's rude.'

'It refers,' said Arthur, with dignity, 'to the bottom of the Swanee River.'

Peter checked up on this with his own granny, who had lasted better than Arthur's, and it was true.

It was necessary to ask such questions because it was very rarely possible to hear the words above the fluffy noises that vibrated up the needle and into the pick-up, in spite of the fact that Arthur religiously dusted each record with a little velvet tuffet before playing it.

'What's that funny buzzing noise in the background?' said Judith.

'Phyllis Dalbey's All-Girl Choir singing "Keep off the Grass",' said Arthur.

Judith's favourite record was anonymous because the label had come off, owing to damp conditions in Arthur's granny's house, but it was easy to identify on account of this, and because it was dappled with spots of green mould.

'Penicillin,' said Arthur.

Judith asked for the green-spotty record every time Arthur had a musical afternoon. It had a yearning, swooning melody and someone was singing, only they never discovered who or what. It sounded like a parrot slowly swallowing a roll of cotton wool.

'*Aye eee aye ehhh ee ah-ha-ha-ha haw*!'

One day they were playing the green-spotty record and Arthur was called away by his mother. While he was out of the room, Peter leaned over, very daring, and moved the little lever on the speed control from 78 to 100, as far as it would go. Instantly the parrot went mad.

'*Ayeeeeeayeehhheeahahahahaweeaaaasssassserrrrhayayayay*!'

Arthur pelted up the stairs and hurled himself at the gramophone, just as the needle came to the end of the groove and began to zip to and fro in the middle.

'Who did that?'

'I did,' said Peter. 'I wanted to see what would happen.'

'You could have ruined it,' said Arthur. 'The pick-up could have flown off at dizzy speed . . .'

'It shouldn't go up to a hundred if it's dangerous,' said Peter. 'Now make it go ever so slow, grunt grunt grunt.'

'I'm not going to play any more,' said Arthur, but as Judith and Peter went downstairs in deepest disgrace, they heard the strains of Arthur's own favourite tune; 'Around the Corner and Under the Tree', sung by Gracie Fields. None of them had any idea what went on around the corner and under the tree, except for one glorious line that had escaped the ravages of time and Arthur's granny.

'He went and sat down on his spurs and oh! he was cut up.'

One day when it was not raining, not even cloudy, Arthur asked them if they wanted to come and hear some music.

'Special music,' said Arthur. He took them indoors, but instead of going upstairs to the attic he led the way into the living-room.

'Your mum doesn't like us coming in here,' said Peter.

'She's out,' said Arthur, briefly. 'Now, look at this.' They looked. On a little table under the window was a black box with a long tail of flex hanging down behind. 'Guess what this is.'

'An electric suitcase,' said Judith.

'I think your budgie's dead,' said Peter.

Arthur felt that he was not being taken seriously.

'It's just sitting on the floor. It likes sitting on the floor,' he said. 'Now, watch.' He lifted the lid of the suitcase and propped it open. Inside was a turntable. 'What do you think of that?'

'Is it broken?' said Peter.

'Broken? Of course it's not broken. It's brand new. We only got it last night,' said Arthur.

'But it's not all there.'

'Of course it's all there. It's a gramophone – can't you see?'

'Yes, but where's the pick-up?' said Judith, missing the long, serpentine chrome tube that they were used to. Arthur placed his finger on the square head of a short plastic bar.

'Here it is.'

'But where's the big round thing at the end?' said Peter. 'Where do you put the needle in? Where are the needles?'

'It doesn't use needles,' Arthur said, triumphantly. 'Look.' He lifted the so-called pick-up and pointed to something that neither of them could see. 'It has a stylus. It's a whole sapphire.'

'What, like in rings and things?' said Judith, searching for a flash of blue fire.

'Yes. It's a precious stone. It's worth several – several *pounds.*'

'Come off it,' said Peter. 'You couldn't afford it.'

'But we've got it,' said Arthur.

'You couldn't afford a new one every time you changed the record.'

'You don't have to change it. It lasts and lasts. It doesn't wear out for years and years and years.'

'I can't even see it,' said Judith.

'It's not there, that's why,' said Peter, peering. 'How'd you get vibrations out with that little thing?'

'It's electric,' said Arthur.

'How'd you wind it up?'

'You don't. It's the electricity makes it go round. You don't have to wind it up. Watch.'

He turned a switch and the turntable began to revolve.

'I bet you wound it up before we came,' said Peter. 'Now put a record on. I bet nothing comes out.'

Arthur had one to hand. He put it on the turntable, switched on again and lowered the pick-up. A high tenor voice began to sing . . . words.

> '*How beautiful they are, the lordly ones,*
> *Who dwell in the hills, in the hollow hills.*
> *They have faces like flowers . . .*'

'I always thought it was frogs,' said Peter, disappointed. 'They have faces like frogs, I thought.'

'Shhh,' said Judith. 'You can really hear him singing.

I didn't realize it was a man. Oh, Arthur' – she had a brilliant idea – 'let's have Green Spotty.'

Arthur took the 'Fairy Song' from the turntable and replaced it with the green-spotty record. He lowered the pick-up.

'*I dreamed that I dwelt in marble halls, with vassals and serfs at my side . . .*'

Judith sat silent and enraptured to the end. Who would have thought that *aye eeee aye ehhh ee ah-ha-ha-ha haw* could mean all that? Peter was still scowling suspiciously at the pick-up.

'I don't believe that it's electricity getting the sound out.'

'Stupid kid,' said Arthur. 'Telephones are electric. TV's electric. Wireless is electric. They make noises.'

'Yes, but this is a record,' said Peter, with faultless logic. 'It's not an electric *record*.'

'All right. Listen to this.' Arthur whipped 'Marble Halls' away with fine disdain and all five fingers on the grooves, grease deposits notwithstanding. From a shelf under the table he brought a record in a stiff cardboard cover.

'It's got a colour picture on it,' said Judith. 'All shiny like a photo. It's one of those dancing ladies.'

'This is Ravel's "Bolero",' said Arthur. 'By Ravel.'

'It looks funny,' said Peter. 'It hasn't got any grooves.'

'It's got very small grooves,' said Arthur. 'It's a long-playing record. It goes on for fifteen minutes.'

'I bet it doesn't.'

'All right then. Watch.'

Arthur put the record on the turntable and set it moving. Then he adjusted a knob at the side and the record stopped spinning and went slower and slower, until they could read the words on the label.

'I know what this'll sound like,' said Peter. 'Grunt grunt grunt.'

The music began. Judith and Peter were so busy reading the words on the label that they failed to notice the progress of the stylus, until Arthur pointed out that after five minutes it was still only a little distance from the edge.

'I told you,' he said, smugly, but this time he had gone too far.

'It's one of your stupid lies,' said Peter. 'You think I'm stupid or something? I'm going home.'

'Stupid kid,' said Arthur. 'You don't know anything. This is a miracle of modern engineering or something. We're getting a tape-recorder next.'

'Ho yes? Electric tape-measure, I suppose,' said Peter, and he was off, out of the room. Judith ran after him.

'Peter – don't be silly. It's working. You can hear it working.'

'Him and his stupid lies,' said Peter, halfway down the front steps. 'I bet it's got a little handle somewhere. Playing records with jewels! Just because he's older . . .'

'But it *did* play.'

They parted company at the foot of the steps, Peter heading for home and the Encyclopaedia.

'Mind you,' he said, over his shoulder. 'If it wasn't Arthur's – I'd believe it.'

8 The Coronation Mob

'They've climbed Everest,' said my mother at breakfast on Coronation morning.

'Who's Everest?' said my brother. He was three. He didn't know about mountains.

'Who's climbed it?' said my father.

'Hillary and Tensing. It's in the paper, look.' She showed us the headline about Mount Everest and the photographs of the men who had climbed it.

'Is that actually them, actually on top of Mount Everest?' I said.

'I doubt it,' said my father. 'They'd be wearing special clothes and oxygen masks, I should think. The air's very thin, so high up.'

'I expect they'd have a flag to plant on top,' said my mother.

My brother drew a picture in the stop-press. He drew a circle with a wavy line coming out of it.

'What a lovely balloon,' said my mother.

'It's the Queen,' said my brother. He coloured the circle with marmalade.

'I thought that wavy line was a bit of string.'

'It's her leg.'

'Don't play with your food,' said my father. 'I think you'll find she has two legs.'

'No she hasn't. She goes hop, hop, hop,' said my brother.

He didn't know much about the Queen, either, because he had never seen her, even on television. There was only one television set on our side of the street. It belonged to the Savilles, three doors down, and everyone in our row was going to watch the Coronation on it; everyone, that is, except my father. He said he had some urgent work to do, but really it was because of Mrs Saville.

'I know you don't like Mrs S,' said my mother, 'but surely you could go down there just this once. It would be worth it, to see the Coronation.'

'No, it wouldn't,' said my father. 'I wouldn't watch the Last Judgment if it meant seeing it on Mrs Saville's TV.'

At ten o'clock my mother and brother and I went along to the Savilles'. There were chairs lined up in their living-room, but children were allowed to sit on the floor at the front; as a treat. It wasn't exactly a treat. The television set looked like a coffin stood on end, and the picture was right at the top.

Horses began to move across the screen, struggling through a blizzard of fizzing white spots. It was raining hard outside and I assumed it must be snowing in London, but Mr Saville said the picture was faulty.

'Gremlins, ha-ha-ha,' said Mr Saville. He took the television set by the shoulders and shook it. The blizzard got worse and the horses disappeared. It was like watching a funeral with a sock over your head.

I wondered how to get out. The room was dark, except for a sort of blue sheet-lightning from the television, and I thought I might crawl away unnoticed, but I was fenced in by a stockade of shins.

Next to me was my friend Barbara, who lived in the end house. Sometimes she was my friend, but not at the moment. I began to squeeze bits of Barbara between my new white sandals and the floor. Barbara squeaked. After a few minutes enough people noticed for my mother to get embarrassed and send me outside. I burrowed between the shins and stamped out of the room, looking cross. It was a terrible disgrace. I was spoiling the Coronation.

In the street the rain had stopped. My white sandals already had shiny grey patches on the toes, so I hop-scotched from puddle to puddle, down the road towards the recreation ground, where rows of flags were snapping in the wind like wet washing. The pub on the corner was called the Star Inn, and its sign was a beautiful golden star that hung from a curly iron bracket. Now the bracket was golden and the star was red white and blue.

The house next to the pub belonged to the dentist. His brass plate was still brass but he had red white and blue flowers in his window-box this summer, instead of dead wallflowers; and a loyal bush in a tub at the top of the steps that ran up to the front door.

There was a tunnel under these steps and someone was sitting in it. It was my other friend, Billy Chapman, wearing the black school cap with an orange peak that made him look like a penguin. He wasn't at the Savilles' house because his mother thought that television was common.

I didn't ask him what he was doing in the tunnel because I knew it was his gateway to stirring adventures. He would go in one end, plain Billy Chapman, and stagger out at the other, riddled with bullets.

'Just been climbing Everest,' said Billy, casually.

'Why aren't you on top, then?' I asked. I thought he ought to be up on the summit, in the porch.

Billy beckoned me into the tunnel.

'Keep your head down,' he said. There wasn't really room to do anything else. I edged in beside him. 'I was on top,' he went on. 'Then I saw the Swaffers coming, so I had to lie low.'

'Where are they?' I said. I noticed that Billy had his shoes on the wrong feet again. His mother was trying to cure his pigeon toes.

'They're lying in wait round the corner of the pub,' said Billy.

'Why don't you run away, then?' I asked, because I knew he would have to in the end and it seemed only sensible to do it now.

'Trust a girl to say that,' said Billy. 'I've got to see this thing through.'

I didn't argue. I knew that he was quoting from one of the manly books that his mother got him from the library, in which the hero always emerged from terrible fights without a scratch on him. None of the heroes in Billy's books was nine years old with pigeon toes, but Billy hadn't noticed that.

A bug-eyed face squinted round the corner and was quickly withdrawn.

'There's Gordon,' said Billy.

'How do you know?'

'It's Gordon's turn for the gas-mask. Norman had it last week.'

Norman and Gordon Swaffer lived in Pudds Cottages, down an alley at the end of our street. Norman was the elder, but Gordon was the brains of the outfit. When he went into battle he used Norman as a gun-limber, a sandbag or a tank-trap; any piece of military hardware that happened to be needed. Their uncle Tom had been a Desert Rat, among other things, and the Swaffers went about dressed in army cast-offs; leather jerkins, khaki gaiters, tin hats, and the gas-mask which they had to share between them. My father said that Montgomery only won at El Alamein because he sent Tom Swaffer on ahead, to frighten the enemy.

I could see the snout of Gordon's gas-mask sticking

out beyond the brickwork. A little higher up was another head, in goggles and a leather helmet. Norman. Evidently Gordon had disguised him as a human being today.

The gas-mask lunged forward and the Swaffers charged round the corner. Uncle Tom hadn't been able to swipe them a machine-gun, so Gordon had to make his own weapons. They were carrying spears; gardening canes, tipped with gramophone needles. Gordon had a box of matches as well, his flame-thrower. Striking them in quick succession, he threw them into the tunnel.

'They're going to smoke us out,' gasped Billy, between gritted teeth. Already he felt the choking vapour invade his lungs, although the wind extinguished the matches almost before they left Gordon's hand.

'Save yourself,' cried Billy, nobly. Norman was blocking his end of the tunnel and he couldn't get out at the other until I did. I stood up and Gordon waved his gramophone needle at me.

'Thass'our tunnel,' he said, removing the gas-mask.

'No it's not,' said Billy. 'It belongs to the dentist. It's his steps.'

Norman said a rude word. 'Spawn,' he said. I don't know why he thought it was rude, but I could tell he did from the way he said it. Also he wrote it on walls: SPORN. Perhaps it just looked rude.

'It's wrong to swear at girls,' said Billy, crawling out of the tunnel.

'Ha, you should know. You're a girl,' said Gordon.

Billy began his manly act, dancing about on his toes, a warrior penguin.

'Geh'ahvit,' said Norman, levelling his spear, and Billy did get out of it, not from fear of Norman, of course, but because he was not allowed to speak to the Swaffers, and going home full of holes would be an admission of guilt.

None of us was allowed to speak to the Swaffers. Our mothers were afraid that we would learn rude words.

Billy knew that a man should defend his honour, but he also knew when to be diplomatic.

'Are you coming to the Coronation party?' he asked.

'Coming to it? Ho, not half we aren't,' said Gordon. 'We're the Coronation Mob. When there's a Coronation we smash it up.'

'You can't be very busy,' I said.

'The Coronation's in London,' said Billy.

'I mean this here Coronation, after dinner,' said Gordon.

There was to be a party that afternoon in the recreation ground, for everyone in our street, but before we could get on with it we had to see Jane Hodgkiss crowned Queen of Sussex Street. All the girls had put their names in a hat to see who would be Queen, and Jane had won. No one had invited Norman and Gordon to draw for the honour of being the Duke of Edinburgh. The mothers said that Pudds Cottages were really part of Essex Avenue, not Sussex Street, and we all knew what a lie that was, because in Essex Avenue the houses weren't even joined together. Our road was terraced, but the houses were not much like Pudds Cottages. Everyone would have been very shocked at the idea of the Swaffers being left out, but they weren't let in, either.

'We'll wop it all up,' said Gordon. 'And the fancy dress, and the tea-party.'

'How?' said Billy. 'There's only two of you and there's hundreds of us.' He meant seventy-three including the scout master who was going to be Archbishop of

Canterbury and crown Queen Jane. 'Our fathers won't let you. They'll call the police.'

Billy's remedy for everthing was calling the police, which was odd in someone who won the war single-handed every day before lunch.

'We got a gang,' said Gordon. He hadn't.

'I say,' said Billy. 'Surely you don't want to spoil things for everyone else?'

'Yus,' said Norman. Billy decided to try some more diplomacy.

'Are you jealous?' he asked, tactfully. 'Do you want to be in the Coronation? I'd let you be Duke of Edinburgh instead of me. Only I'm not Duke of Edinburgh,' he added.

'No, you're Winston Churchill,' said Gordon.

'I know,' said Billy. 'I'll fight you for it. Fair fight, mind. No kicking. If I win, you must swear not to smash up the Coronation.'

Gordon lay down on the pavement and pretended to die laughing. If I had been Billy I'd have taken this opportunity to jump on Gordon, but Billy was put out by this unsporting reply to his challenge.

'I'll kill y' by meself,' Norman offered helpfully. 'I'll pull y'apart.'

At that moment, Mrs Chapman appeared in her front garden. Television wasn't the only thing that she considered common, but when she was angry, she stood at the gate with her hands on her hips, like anyone else's mother.

'Oh heck,' murmured Billy. This was the worst word he knew, in spite of talking to the Swaffers. He stepped over the dying Gordon and started for home. I walked with him to provide moral support.

'This is serious,' said Billy. He meant the Coronation Mob, not his mother, though I didn't agree with him there. 'We've got to save the Coronation,' he said, thumping palm with fist. 'We must warn everyone, so they'll be ready.'

'Does your mother know where you've been?' demanded Mrs Chapman, as she hauled Billy indoors. That was all she ever said to me. That and, 'Don't pick our privet,' when I was only looking for caterpillars.

All through our Coronation a wet wind scoured the awning above the throne, but when the crown was on, a ray of sunlight shone down just where Queen Jane was standing. That bit got into the *Kentish Express*: SUN SHINES ON SUSSEX STREET QUEEN.

Billy and I stood at the back of the crowd, keeping an eye open for a sight of the gas-mask among the horse-radish leaves that bordered the recreation ground.

'They're getting ready to do a mad rush, later on,' said Billy. 'When they think no one's expecting it.'

We were all lined up for the fancy-dress parade. Billy was Lord Nelson with a patch over one eye, which impaired his efficiency as a look-out, although he had a telescope. My brother was done up as a frog, in long underwear dyed green, with a buckram mask from Woolworths. We couldn't get a frog mask so my mother bought a monkey mask, steamed it over the kettle and pinched it into frog shape. I was the Spirit of England, in bits of butter-muslin dyed red white and blue.

'She looks like the Spirit of Being Hard Up,' said my father. He was going up and down the lines of children, finding out what everyone was supposed to be. This was just as well since it was rather hard to guess, in some cases. Several people pointed out my brother as that dear little dragon.

'Tell them you're a frog,' my mother kept hissing, so

he did, but inside the frog skin he was probably being a train.

We all had to walk past the judges' table, little ones first. My brother went by, legs going up and down like pistons. I was right; he was being a train. Then Christopher Saville, with his head in a box.

'A television set,' my father called out, for the judges' benefit. 'A shepherdess, the Queen of Hearts, a hot – no, surely not – yes, a hot-water bottle.' It was my turn. 'The Spirit of England.'

As I passed the table I saw the gas-mask peering through the horseradish leaves. I left the line and ran over to my father.

'The Coronation Mob's here,' I said. Billy had told him all about it beforehand. I looked round for Billy and by good luck he was busy walking the quarter-deck.

'Lord Nelson,' shouted my father. 'Hang on a moment.' He walked over to the horseradish and addressed the gas-mask.

'What a way to come to a party.'

'Spawn,' said Norman, behind another leaf. Billy came cantering up, waving his telescope.

'Sir, Sir!' My father didn't like being called 'Sir' away from school, but Billy wouldn't learn. 'Sir, they're going to smash us up.'

'Go away,' said my father. He dragged the Coronation Mob out of the horseradish. They were in full battledress: gas-mask, goggles, gaiters, helmet, boots and jerkins, spears at the trail. They reminded me of something, but I couldn't think what. My father could. He yanked a Union Jack off the back of the throne and hung it on Gordon's gramophone needle. Then he took the Mob, one in each hand, and tacked them onto the end of the fancy-dress parade. As they went past the judges he called out, 'Hillary and Tensing on top of

Mount Everest.' There was a tremendous cheer and Norman and Gordon won first prize for the most original costume.

Norman's prize was a moneybox shaped like a crown and Gordon got an autograph book with the Queen on the cover.

'Though what you'll do with it I don't know,' said my

father. 'I imagine most of your heroes are in the Chamber of Horrors.'

The Coronation Mob wouldn't stay for tea, and left as soon as they could.

'They're not a bit grateful,' complained Billy, watching them go. Gordon was already converting Norman's moneybox into an offensive weapon.

'Of course they aren't,' said my father. 'They came to smash us up and then I went and made them win first prize.'

'You should have smashed them up, Sir,' said Billy, regretfully.

'Why?' said my father. 'They're not exactly a threat to civilization as we know it. What did you want, a massacre?' Billy gave him a headache. I think he preferred the Coronation Mob, even if they did come from Pudds Cottages.

As it happened, the Mob left off being a mob soon afterwards. That autumn Gordon started at the Grammar School, and after that we didn't get the chance not to speak to him.

He wouldn't speak to us.

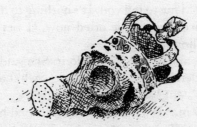

9 Send Three and Fourpence We are Going to a Dance

Mike and Ruth Dixon got on well enough, but not so well that they wanted to walk home from school together. Ruth would not have minded, but Mike, who was two classes up, preferred to amble along with his friends so that he usually arrived a long while after Ruth did.

Ruth was leaning out of the kitchen window when he came in through the side gate, kicking a brick.

'I've got a message for you,' said Mike. 'From school. Miss Middleton wants you to go and see her tomorrow before assembly, and take a dead frog.'

'What's she want *me* to take a dead frog for?' said Ruth. 'She's not my teacher. I haven't got a dead frog.'

'How should I know?' Mike let himself in. 'Where's Mum?'

'Round Mrs Todd's. Did she really say a dead frog? I mean, really say it?'

'Derek told me to tell you. It's nothing to do with me.'

Ruth cried easily. She cried now. 'I bet she never. You're pulling my leg.'

'I'm not, and you'd better do it. She said it was important – Derek said – and you know what a rotten old temper she's got,' said Mike, feelingly.

'But why me? It's not fair.' Ruth leaned her head on the window-sill and wept in earnest. 'Where'm I going to find a dead frog?'

'Well, you can peel them off the road sometimes, when they've been run over. They go all dry and flat, like pressed flowers,' said Mike. He did think it a trifle unreasonable to demand dead frogs from little girls, but Miss Middleton *was* unreasonable. Everyone knew that. 'You could start a pressed frog collection,' he said.

Ruth sniffed fruitily. 'What do you think Miss'll do if I don't get one?'

'She'll go barmy, that's what,' said Mike. 'She's barmy anyway,' he said. 'Nah, don't start howling again. Look, I'll go down the ponds after tea. I know there's frogs there because I saw the spawn, back at Easter.'

'But those frogs are alive. She wants a dead one.'

'I dunno. Perhaps we could get it put to sleep or something, like Mrs Todd's Tibby was. And don't tell Mum. She doesn't like me down the ponds and she won't let us have frogs indoors. Get an old box with a lid and leave it on the rockery, and I'll put old Froggo in it when I come home. *And stop crying!*'

After Mike had gone out Ruth found the box that her summer sandals had come in. She poked air holes in the top and furnished it with damp grass and a tin lid full of water. Then she left it on the rockery with a length of darning wool so that Froggo could be fastened down safely until morning. It was only possible to imagine Froggo alive; all tender and green and saying croak-croak. She could not think of him dead and flat and handed over to Miss Middleton, who definitely must have gone barmy. Perhaps Mike or Derek had been wrong about the dead part. She hoped they had.

She was in the bathroom, getting ready for bed, when Mike came home. He looked round the door and stuck up his thumbs.

'Operation Frog successful. Over and out.'

'Wait. Is he . . . alive?'

'Shhh. Mum's in the hall. Yes.'

'What's he like?'

'Sort of frog-shaped. Look, I've got him; O.K.? I'm going down now.'

'Is he green.'

'No. More like that pork pie that went mouldy on top. Good night!'

Mike had hidden Froggo's dungeon under the front hedge, so all Ruth had to do next morning was scoop it up as she went out of the gate. Mike had left earlier with his friends, so she paused for a moment to introduce herself. She tapped quietly on the lid. 'Hullo?'

There was no answering cry of croak-croak. Perhaps he *was* dead. Ruth felt a tear coming and raised the lid a fraction at one end. There was a scrabbling noise and at the other end of the box she saw something small and alive, crouching in the grass.

'Poor Froggo,' she whispered through the air holes. 'I won't let her kill you, I promise,' and she continued on her way to school feeling brave and desperate, and ready to protect Froggo's life at the cost of her own.

The school hall was in the middle of the building and classrooms opened off it. Miss Middleton had Class 3 this year, next to the cloakroom. Ruth hung up her blazer, untied the wool from Froggo's box, and went to meet her doom. Miss Middleton was arranging little stones in an aquarium on top of the bookcase, and jerked her head when Ruth knocked, to show that she should come in.

'I got him, Miss,' said Ruth, holding out the shoe box in trembling hands.

'What, dear?' said Miss Middleton, up to her wrists in water-weed.

'Only he's not dead and I won't let you kill him!' Ruth cried, and swept off the lid with a dramatic flourish. Froggo, who must have been waiting for this,

sprung out, towards Miss Middleton, landed with a clammy sound on that vulnerable place between the collar bones, and slithered down inside Miss Middleton's blouse.

Miss Middleton taught Nature Study. She was not afraid of little damp creatures, but she was not expecting Froggo. She gave a squawk of alarm and jumped backwards. The aquarium skidded in the opposite direction; took off; shattered against a desk. The contents broke over Ruth's new sandals in a tidal wave, and Lily the goldfish thrashed about in a shallow puddle on the floor. People came running with mops and dustpans. Lily Fish was taken out by the tail to recover in the cloakroom sink. Froggo was arrested while trying to leave Miss Middleton's blouse through the gap between two buttons, and put back in his box with a weight on top in case he made another dash for freedom.

Ruth, crying harder than she had ever done in her life, was sent to stand outside the Headmaster's room, accused of playing stupid practical jokes; and cruelty to frogs.

Sir looked rather as if he had been laughing, but it seemed unlikely, under the circumstances, and Ruth's eyes were so swollen and tear-filled that she couldn't see clearly. He gave her a few minutes to dry out and then said,

'This isn't like you, Ruth. Whatever possessed you to go throwing frogs at poor Miss Middleton? And poor frog, come to that.'

'She told me to bring her a frog,' said Ruth, stanching another tear at the injustice of it all. 'Only she wanted a dead one, and I couldn't find a dead one, and I couldn't kill Froggo. I won't kill him,' she said, remembering her vow on the way to school.

'Miss Middleton says she did not ask you to bring her a frog, or kill her a frog. She thinks you've been very foolish and unkind,' said Sir, 'and I think you are not telling the truth. Now . . .'

'Mike told me to,' said Ruth.

'Your brother? Oh, come now.'

'He did. He said Miss Middleton wanted me to go to her before assembly with a dead frog and I did, only it wasn't dead and I won't!'

'Ruth! Don't grizzle. No one is going to murder your frog, but we must get this nonsense sorted out.' Sir opened his door and called to a passer-by, 'Tell Michael Dixon that I want to see him at once, in my office.'

Mike arrived, looking wary. He had heard the crash and kept out of the way, but a summons from Sir was not to be ignored.

'Come in, Michael,' said Sir. 'Now, why did you tell your sister that Miss Middleton wanted her to bring a dead frog to school?'

'It wasn't me,' said Mike. 'It was a message from Miss Middleton.'

'Miss Middleton told you?'

'No, Derek Bingham told me. She told him to tell me – I suppose,' said Mike, sulkily. He scowled at Ruth. All her fault.

'Then you'd better fetch Derek Bingham here right away. We're going to get to the bottom of this.'

Derek arrived. He too had heard the crash.

'Come in, Derek,' said Sir. 'I understand that you told Michael here some tarradiddle about his sister. You let him think it was a message from Miss Middleton, didn't you?'

'Yes, well . . .' Derek shuffled. 'Miss Middleton didn't tell *me*. She told, er, someone, and they told me.'

'Who was this someone?'

Derek turned all noble and stood up straight and pale. 'I can't remember, Sir.'

'Don't let's have any heroics about sneaking, Derek, or I shall get very *cross*.'

Derek's nobility ebbed rapidly. 'It was Tim Hancock, Sir. He said Miss Middleton wanted Ruth Dixon to bring her a dead dog before assembly.'

'A dead *dog*?'

'Yes Sir.'

'Didn't you think it a bit strange that Miss Middleton should ask Ruth for a dead dog, Derek?'

'I thought she must have one, Sir.'

'But why should Miss Middleton want it?'

'Well, she does do Nature Study,' said Derek.

'Go and fetch Tim,' said Sir.

Tim had been playing football on the field when the aquarium went down. He came in with an innocent smile which wilted when he saw what was waiting for him.

'Sir?'

'Would you mind repeating the message that you gave Derek yesterday afternoon?'

'I told him Miss Middleton wanted Sue Nixon to bring her a red sock before assembly,' said Tim. 'It was important.'

'Red sock? Sue Nixon?' said Sir. He was beginning to look slightly wild-eyed. 'Who's Sue Nixon? There's no one in this school called Sue Nixon.'

'I don't know any of the girls, Sir,' said Tim.

'Didn't you think a red sock was an odd thing to ask for?'

'I thought she was bats, Sir.'

'Sue Nixon?'

'No Sir. Miss Middleton, Sir,' said truthful Tim.

Sir raised his eyebrows. 'But why did you tell Derek?'

'I couldn't find anyone else, Sir. It was late.'

'But why Derek?'

'I had to tell someone or I'd have got into trouble,' said Tim, virtuously.

'You are in trouble,' said Sir. 'Michael, ask Miss Middleton to step in here for a moment, please.'

Miss Middleton, frog-ridden, looked round the door.

'I'm sorry to bother you again,' said Sir, 'but it seems

that Tim thinks you told him that one Sue Nixon was to bring you a red sock before assembly.'

'Tim!' said Miss Middleton, very shocked. 'That's a naughty fib. I never told you any such thing.'

'Oh Sir,' said Tim. 'Miss didn't tell me. It was Pauline Bates done that.'

'*Did* that. I think I see Pauline out in the hall,' said Sir. 'In the P.T. class. Yes? Let's have her in.'

Pauline was very small and very frightened. Sir sat her on his knee and told her not to worry. 'All we want to know,' he said, 'is what you said to Tim yesterday. About Sue Nixon and the dead dog.'

'Red sock, Sir,' said Tim.

'Sorry. Red sock. Well, Pauline?'

Pauline looked as if she might join Ruth in tears. Ruth had just realized that she was no longer involved, and was crying with relief.

'You said Miss Middleton gave you a message for Sue Nixon. What was it?'

'It wasn't Sue Nixon,' said Pauline, damply. 'It was June Nichols. It wasn't Miss Middleton, it was Miss Wimbledon.'

'There *is* no Miss Wimbledon,' said Sir. 'June Nichols, yes. I know June, but Miss Wimbledon . . . ?'

'She means Miss Wimpole, Sir,' said Tim. 'The big girls call her Wimbledon 'cause she plays tennis, Sir, in a little skirt.'

'I thought you didn't know any girls,' said Sir. 'What did Miss Wimpole say to you, Pauline?'

'She didn't,' said Pauline. 'It was Moira Thatcher. She said to tell June Nichols to come and see Miss Whatsit before assembly and bring her bed socks.'

'Then why tell Tim?'

'I couldn't find June. June's in his class.'

'I begin to see daylight,' said Sir. 'Not much, but

it's there. All right, Pauline. Go and get Moira, please.'

Moira had recently had a new brace fitted across her front teeth. It caught the light when she opened her mouth.

'Yeth, Thir?'

'Moira, take it slowly, and tell us what the message was about June Nichols.'

Moira took a deep breath and polished the brace with her tongue.

'Well, Thir, Mith Wimpole thaid to thell June to thee her before athembly with her wed fw – thw – thth –'

'Frock?' said Sir. Moira nodded gratefully. 'So why tell Pauline?'

'Pauline liveth up her thtweet, Thir.'

'No I don't,' said Pauline. 'They moved. They got a council house, up the Ridgeway.'

'All right, Moira,' said Sir. 'Just ask Miss Wimpole if she could thp – spare me a minute of her time, please?'

If Miss Wimpole was surprised to find eight people in Sir's office, she didn't show it. As there was no longer room to get inside, she stood at the doorway and waved. Sir waved back. Mike instantly decided that Sir fancied Miss Wimpole.

'Miss Wimpole, I believe you must be the last link in the chain. Am I right in thinking that you wanted June Nichols to see you before assembly, with her red frock?'

'Why, yes,' said Miss Wimpole. 'She's dancing a solo at the end-of-term concert. I wanted her to practise, but she didn't turn up.'

'Thank you,' said Sir. 'One day, when we both have a spare hour or two, I'll tell you why she didn't turn up. As for you lot,' he said, turning to the mob round his desk, 'you seem to have been playing Chinese Whispers without knowing it. You also seem to think that the

106

entire staff is off its head. You may be right. I don't know. Red socks, dead dogs, live frogs – we'll put your friend in the school pond, Ruth. Fetch him at break. And now, someone had better find June Nichols and deliver Miss Wimpole's message.'

'Oh, there's no point, Sir. She couldn't have come anyway,' said Ruth. 'She's got chicken-pox. She hasn't been at school for ages.'

10 Nule

The house was not old enough to be interesting, just old enough to be starting to fall apart. The few interesting things had been dealt with ages ago, when they first moved in. There was a bell-push in every room, somehow connected to a glass case in the kitchen which contained a list of names and an indicator which wavered from name to name when a button was pushed, before settling on one of them: *Parlour*; *Drawing Room*; *Master Bedroom*; *Second Bedroom*; *Back Bedroom*.

'What are they for?' said Libby one morning, after roving round the house and pushing all the buttons in turn. At that moment Martin pushed the button in the front room and the indicator slid up to *Parlour*, vibrating there while the bell rang. And rang and rang.

'To fetch up the maid,' said Mum.

'We haven't got a maid.'

'No, but you've got me,' said Mum, and tied an old sock over the bell, so that afterwards it would only whirr instead of ringing.

The mouse-holes in the kitchen looked interesting, too. The mice were bold and lounged about, making no effort at all to be timid and mouse-like. They sat on the draining board in the evenings and could scarcely be bothered to stir themselves when the light was switched on.

'Easy living has made them soft,' said Mum. 'They have a gaming-hell behind the boiler. They throw dice all day. They dance the can-can at night.'

'Come off it,' said Dad. 'You'll be finding crates of tiny gin bottles, next.'

'They dance the can-can,' Mum insisted. 'Right over my head they dance it. I can hear them. If you didn't sleep so soundly, you'd hear them too.'

'Oh, that. That's not mice,' said Dad, with a cheery smile. 'That's rats.'

Mum minded the mice less than the bells, until the day she found footprints in the frying-pan.

'Sorry, lads, the party's over,' she said to the mice, who were no doubt combing the dripping from their elegant whiskers at that very moment, and the mouse-holes were blocked up.

Dad did the blocking-up, and also some unblocking, so that after the bath no longer filled itself through the plug hole, the house stopped being interesting altogether; for a time.

Libby and Martin did what they could to improve matters. Beginning in the cupboard under the stairs, they worked their way through the house, up to the attic, looking for something; anything; tapping walls and floors, scouring cupboards, measuring and calculating, but there were no hidden cavities, no secret doors, no ambiguous bulges under the wallpaper, except where the damp got in. The cupboard below the stairs was full of old pickle jars, and what they found in the attic didn't please anyone, least of all Dad.

'That's dry rot,' he said. 'Thank god this isn't our house,' and went cantering off to visit the estate agents, Tench and Tench, in the High Street. Dad called them Shark and Shark. As he got to the gate he turned back and yelled, 'The Plague! The Plague! Put a red cross on the door!' which made Mrs Bowen, over the fence, lean right out of her landing window instead of hiding behind the curtains.

When Dad came back from the estate agents he was growling.

'Shark junior says that since the whole row is coming down inside two years, it isn't worth bothering about. I understand that the new by-pass is going to run right through the scullery.'

'What did Shark senior say?' said Mum.

'I didn't see him. I've never seen him. I don't believe that there is a Shark senior,' said Dad. 'I think he's dead. I think Young Shark keeps him in a box under the bed.'

'Don't be nasty,' said Mum, looking at Libby who worried about things under the bed even in broad daylight. 'I just hope we find a house of our own before this place collapses on our heads – and we shan't be buying it from the Sharks.'

She went back to her sewing, not in a good mood. The mice had broken out again. Libby went into the kitchen to look for them. Martin ran upstairs, rhyming:

> *Mr Shark,*
> *In the dark,*
> *Under the bed.*
> *Dead.'*

When he came down again, Mum was putting away the sewing and Libby was parading around the hall in a pointed hat with a veil and a long red dress that looked rich and splendid unless you knew, as Martin did, that it was made of old curtains.

The hall was dark in the rainy summer afternoon, and Libby slid from shadow to shadow, rustling.

'What are you meant to be?' said Martin. 'An old witch?'

'I'm the Sleeping Beauty's mother,' said Libby, and lowering her head she charged along the hall, pointed hat foremost, like a unicorn.

110

Martin changed his mind about walking downstairs and slid down the bannisters instead. He suspected that he would not be allowed to do this for much longer. Already the bannister rail creaked, and who knew where the dreaded dry rot would strike next? As he reached the upright post at the bottom of the stairs, Mum came out of the back room, lugging the sewing-machine, and just missed being impaled on Libby's hat.

'Stop rushing up and down,' said Mum. 'You'll ruin those clothes and I've only just finished them. Go and take them off. And you,' she said, turning to Martin, 'stop swinging on that newel post. Do you want to tear it up by the roots?'

The newel post was supposed to be holding up the bannisters, but possibly it was the other way about. At the foot it was just a polished wooden post, but further up it had been turned on a lathe, with slender hips, a waist, a bust almost, and square shoulders. On top was a round ball, as big as a head.

There was another at the top of the stairs but it had lost its head. Dad called it Ann Boleyn; the one at the bottom was simply a newel post, but Libby thought that this too was its name; Nule Post, like Ann Boleyn or Libby Anderson.

Mrs Nule Post.

Lady Nule Post.

When she talked to it she just called it Nule.

The pointed hat and the old curtains were Libby's costume for the school play. Martin had managed to stay out of the school play, but he knew all of Libby's lines by heart as she chanted them round the house, up and down stairs, in a strained, jerky voice, one syllable per step.

'My-dear-we-must-in-vite-all-the-fair-ies-to-the-chris-ten-ing, Hullo, Nule, we-will-not-in-vite-the-wick-ed-fair-y!'

On the last day of term, he sat with Mum and Dad in the school hall and watched Libby go through the same routine on stage. She was word-perfect, in spite of speaking as though her shock absorbers had collapsed, but as most of the cast spoke the same way it didn't sound so very strange.

Once the holidays began Libby went back to talking like Libby, although she still wore the pointed hat and the curtains, until they began to drop to pieces. The curtains went for dusters, but the pointed hat was around for a long time until Mum picked it up and threatened, 'Take this thing away or it goes in the dustbin.'

Libby shunted up and down stairs a few times with the hat on her head, and then Mum called out that Jane-next-door had come to play. If Libby had been at the top of the stairs, she might have left the hat on her bed, but she was almost at the bottom so she plonked it down on Nule's cannon-ball head, and went out to fight Jane over whose turn it was to kidnap the teddy-bear. She hoped it was Jane's turn. If Libby were the kidnapper, she would have to sit about for ages holding Teddy to ransom behind the water tank, while Jane galloped round the garden on her imaginary pony, whacking the hydrangea bushes with a broomstick.

The hat definitely did something for Nule. When Martin came in later by the front door, he thought at first that it was a person standing at the foot of the stairs. He had to look twice before he understood who it was. Mum saw it at the same time.

'I told Libby to put that object away or I'd throw it in the dustbin.'

'Oh, don't,' said Martin. 'Leave it for Dad to see.'

So she left it, but Martin began to get ideas. The hat made the rest of Nule look very undressed, so he fetched down the old housecoat that had been hanging behind the bathroom door when they moved in. It was purple, with blue paisleys swimming all over it, and very worn, as though it had been somebody's favourite housecoat. The sleeves had set in creases around arms belonging to someone they had never known.

Turning it front to back, he buttoned it like a bib round Nule's neck so that it hung down to the floor. He filled two gloves with screwed-up newspaper, poked them into the sleeves and pinned them there. The weight made the arms dangle and opened the creases. He put a pair of football boots under the hem of the housecoat with the toes just sticking out, and stood back to see how it looked.

As he expected, in the darkness of the hall it looked just like a person, waiting, although there was something not so much lifelike as deathlike in the hang of those dangling arms.

Mum and Libby first saw Nule as they came out of the kitchen together.

'Who on earth did this?' said Mum as they drew alongside.

'It wasn't me,' said Libby, and sounded very glad that it wasn't.

'It was you left the hat, wasn't it?'

'Yes, but not the other bits.'

'What do you think?' said Martin.

'Horrible thing,' said Mum, but she didn't ask him to take it down. Libby sidled round Nule and ran upstairs as close to the wall as she could get.

When Dad came home from work he stopped in the doorway and said, 'Hullo – who's that? Who . . . ?' before Martin put the light on and showed him.

'An idol, I suppose,' said Dad. 'Nule, god of dry rot,' and he bowed low at the foot of the stairs. At the same time the hat slipped forward slightly, as if Nule had lowered its head in acknowledgement. Martin also bowed low before reaching up to put the hat straight.

Mum and Dad seemed to think that Nule was rather funny, so it stayed at the foot of the stairs. They never bowed to it again, but Martin did, every time he went upstairs, and so did Libby. Libby didn't talk to Nule any more, but she watched it a lot. One day she said, 'Which way is it facing?'

'Forwards, of course,' said Martin, but it was hard to tell unless you looked at the feet. He drew two staring eyes and a toothy smile on a piece of paper and cut them out. They were attached to the front of Nule's head with little bits of chewing-gum.

'That's better,' said Libby, laughing, and next time she went upstairs she forgot to bow. Martin was not so sure. Nule looked ordinary now, just like a newel post wearing a housecoat, football boots and the Sleeping Beauty's mother's hat. He took off the eyes and the mouth and rubbed away the chewing-gum.

'*That's* better,' he said, while Nule stared once more without eyes, and smiled without a mouth.

Libby said nothing.

At night the house creaked.

'Thiefly footsteps,' said Libby.

'It's the furniture warping,' said Mum.

Libby thought she said that the furniture was walking, and she could well believe it. The dressing-table had feet with claws; why shouldn't it walk in the dark, tugging fretfully this way and that because the clawed feet pointed in opposite directions? The bath had feet too. Libby imagined it galloping out of the bathroom and tobogganing downstairs on its stomach, like a great white walrus plunging into the sea. If someone held the door open, it would whizz up the path and crash into the front gate. If someone held the gate open, it would shoot across the road and hit the district nurse's car, which she parked under the street light, opposite.

Libby thought of headlines in the local paper – NURSE RUN OVER BY BATH – and giggled, until she heard the creaks again. Then she hid under the bed-clothes.

In his bedroom Martin heard the creaks too, but he had a different reason for worrying. In the attic where the dry rot lurked, there was a big oak wardrobe full of old dead ladies' clothes. It was directly over his head. Supposing it came through?

Next day he moved the bed.

The vacuum cleaner had lost its casters and had to be helped, by Libby pushing from behind. It skidded up the hall and knocked Nule's football boots askew.

'The Hoover doesn't like Nule either,' said Libby. Although she wouldn't talk to Nule anymore she liked talking *about* it, as though that somehow made Nule safer.

'What's that?' said Mum.

'It knocked Nule's feet off.'

'Well, put them back,' said Mum, but Libby preferred not to. When Martin came in he set them side by side, but later they were kicked out of place again. If people began to complain that Nule was in the way, Nule would have to go. He got round this by putting the right boot where the left had been and the left boot on the bottom stair. When he left it, the veil on the hat was hanging down behind, but as he went upstairs after tea he noticed that it was now draped over Nule's right

shoulder, as if Nule had turned its head to see where its feet were going.

That night the creaks were louder than ever, like a burglar on hefty tiptoe. Libby had mentioned thieves only that evening, and Mum had said, 'What have we got worth stealing?'

Martin felt fairly safe because he had worked out that if the wardrobe fell tonight, it would land on his chest of drawers and not on him, but what might it not bring down with it? Then he realized that the creaks were coming not from above but from below.

He held his breath. Downstairs didn't creak.

His alarm clock gleamed greenly in the dark and told him that it had gone two o'clock. Mum and Dad were asleep ages ago. Libby would sooner burst than leave her bed in the dark. Perhaps it *was* a burglar. Feeling noble and reckless he put on the bedside lamp, slid out of bed, trod silently across the carpet. He turned on the main light and opened the door. The glow shone out of the doorway and saw him as far as the landing light switch at the top of the stairs, but he never had time to turn it on. From the top of the stairs he could look down into the hall where the street light opposite shone coldly through the frosted panes of the front door.

It shone on the hall stand where the coats hung, on the blanket chest and the brass jug that stood on it, through the white coins of the honesty plants in the brass jug, and on the broody telephone that never rang at night. It did not shine on Nule. Nule was not there.

Nule was halfway up the stairs, one hand on the bannisters and one hand holding up the housecoat, clear of its boots. The veil on the hat drifted like smoke across the frosted glass of the front door. Nule creaked and came up another step.

Martin turned and fled back to the bedroom, and dived under the bedclothes, just like Libby who was three years younger and believed in ghosts.

'Were you reading in bed last night?' said Mum, prodding him awake next morning. Martin came out from under the pillow, very slowly.

'No, Mum.'

'You went to sleep with the light on. *Both* lights,' she said, leaning across to switch off the one by the bed.

'I'm sorry.'

'Perhaps you'd like to pay the next electricity bill?'

Mum had brought him a cup of tea, which meant that she had been down to the kitchen and back again, unscathed. Martin wanted to ask her if there was anything strange on the stairs, but he didn't quite know how to put it. He drank the tea, dressed, and went along the landing.

He looked down into the hall where the sun shone through the frosted glass of the front door, onto the hall-stand, the blanket chest, the honesty plants in the brass jug, and the telephone that began to ring as he looked at it. It shone on Nule, standing with its back to him at the foot of the stairs.

Mum came out of the kitchen to answer the phone and Martin went down and stood three steps up, watching Nule and waiting for Mum to finish talking. Nule looked just as it always did. Both feet were back on ground level, side by side.

'I wish you wouldn't hang about like that when I'm on the phone,' said Mum, putting down the receiver and turning round. 'Eavesdropper. Breakfast will be ready in five minutes.'

She went back into the kitchen and Martin sat on the blanket chest, looking at Nule. It was time for Nule to go. He should walk up to Nule this minute, kick away the boots, rip off the housecoat, throw away the hat, but . . .

He stayed where he was, watching the motionless football boots, the dangling sleeves. The breeze from an open window stirred the hem of the housecoat and revealed the wooden post beneath, rooted firmly in the floor as it had been for seventy years.

There were no feet in the boots; no arms in the sleeves.

If he destroyed Nule, it would mean that he *believed* that he had seen Nule climbing the stairs last night, but if he left Nule alone, Nule might walk again.

He had a problem.

UNDER THE AUTUMN GARDEN

They were studying local history at school, and since Matthew was head boy, he felt he ought to do a really good project. He knew that his garden lay over the remains of an old priory, so why not dig it up and see what exciting relics he could discover? But his idea turns sour as all kinds of people interfere. He would never even have started if he'd known the obstacles before him!

THUNDER AND LIGHTNINGS

Victor was the oddest boy Andrew had ever met. How could he be so dim in school, and yet know so much about aeroplanes? But as their friendship grew, Andrew became more and more concerned about what would happen when Victor discovered that the Lightnings he loved so much were all to be scrapped.

HAIRS IN THE PALM OF THE HAND

Two sharp school stories: the first about a class wager on how much time can be wasted in a week; the second about an intruder who causes infinite disruption during a day in a comprehensive.

MAN IN MOTION

His sister had had friends in. How had she managed to make so many so fast? Lloyd had the school, the friends were all left behind in Hampshire. Once Lloyd has started at his new school, however, he soon finds he's playing cricket with Salman, swimming with Kenneth, cycling with James and playing badminton with Vlad. But American football is Lloyd's greatest enthusiasm, and in time it tests his loyalties, not only to his other sporting activities, but also to the new friends he shares them with.

HANDLES

Stuck miles from anywhere with her boring relations, Erica's holiday is far from lovely. But then she discovers the smallest industrial estate in the world where she can indulge her love of motor-bikes among a bunch of characters with the unlikely 'handles' of Elsie, Bunny and the Gremlin. Erica longs to be accepted by them, but she has to have a 'handle' too – and Elsie is the only one who can bestow it.

TROUBLE HALF-WAY

Amy knew her worrying sometimes drove Richard mad, but she did have plenty to worry about. Grandad was in hospital so Mum had gone with baby Helen to look after Grandma and left Amy with a new stepfather she still felt awkward with. Worse still, Richard wanted to take her Up North delivering some furniture in his lorry. Of course, it *might* be fun doing something so unfamiliar, but Amy wasn't going to start enjoying it without doing her fair share of worrying first.

DREAM HOUSE

For Hannah, West Stenning Manor is a place for day-dreams, but for Dina its attraction lies in the celebrities who tutor the courses there. But when a well-known actor arrives, hotly pursued by his attention-seeking daughter Julia, Dina begins to realize that famous people are no better than ordinary ones. A warm and tremendously funny story.